Caroline has managed to fit a long and wobbly path into her 44 years, which started as the daughter of Irish immigrant parents in West Ham, London and migrating to Basildon along with the Ford tractor plant.

Roles she has taken on the journey so far have been as, mother to three vibrant and interesting children, a nurse and a social worker. She has now decided to put her overactive imagination to the test as a writer.

Caroline has a great desire to travel the world as much as possible and a love of art on which to base the travels. She hopes that her new career as a writer has only just begun, as she has many more tales to tell.

FORMATION FLYING

Caroline Clare

FORMATION FLYING

Vanguard Press

A CIP catalogue record for this title is
available from the British Library.

ISBN 978 1 84386 388 5

*Vanguard Press is an imprint of
Pegasus Elliot MacKenzie Publishers Ltd.*
www.pegasuspublishers.com

First Published in 2007

**Vanguard Press
Sheraton House Castle Park
Cambridge England**

Printed & Bound in Great Britain

Writer's Disclaimer

This book is purely a work of fiction. Any reference to any persons, places, historical events or recipe for cake should be treated as highly suspicious and should not be actioned upon without further reference to a more reliable source. Any similarities to either persons or places in reality is probably intentional although basically a bunch of twaddle, based on no more knowledge than can be accrued from the pages of celebrity magazines on any given week.

Please do not try to create any experiments at home based on information contained in this book.
There are no hidden messages... Even if you read it backwards!

Dedication

With Thanks to
My three little piglets Helen Kevin and
Victoria for their encouragement, support
and love, Alastair My Teddy bear, tower of
strength and support to whom I owe so
much, HRH Maggie for keeping me insane,
Jason for his encouragement and proof
reading, to Herbie thighs Fnar, to all the life
begins at 40 chatters on AOL who have
shown such a wonderful mix of
encouragement and indifference, to so
many friends who have encouraged me to
keep on at it.
Special thanks to Christian and Russell for
the Front cover, Kuru rocks!
Thank you to Pegasus publishing, for
finding me.

chapter one

Form is the kind of bloke who causes a reaction from the majority of people who come across him. Unfortunately the reaction he causes is usually a wrinkling of the nose and an upward movement of the top lip, sort of the face one would pull when unexpectedly confronted with an obnoxious odour. Not that Form smelt, indeed not, Form was meticulous about his personal hygiene.

Really it is hard to say why he caused this reaction. His clothes did always seem to be just a smidgen too small, but that wasn't it. His hair was thinning and what was left of it seemed to be being blown as if he were facing into a wind tunnel, which no one else could feel. But that wasn't it either. Form's voice was sort of pinched and nasally, but that couldn't be it as the reaction often came when Form had not spoken a word. I think it had to be Form's nasal hair, which made his nostrils look like there was a woodlouse or some thing stuck up his nose. That definitely was an off-putting aspect of his features. Come to think of it, he had quite a few off-putting aspects. Anyway, the point is most people assumed they would dislike Form as soon as they saw him, and many of them were right.

Form worked for the local council as the supervisor of the timetabling department. He was known to be pernickety. He loved rules and never was known to as much as bend any, even for himself. It was suspected that he was responsible for the police catching one of the administration team for drink driving after the Christmas bash, as Form had commented on whether the clerk should have that glass of champagne when he was on antibiotics. Form did not even notice that no one was speaking to him for over a month after that. Actually, in the most part, Form was totally unaware that people in general didn't like him. He had no wish to be popular, and he assumed that unless someone confronted him, everyone else was as indifferent to him as he was to them.

However Form did not go totally unappreciated by his work colleagues. Most of the new people would at some time comment about him, only to be told by others who had worked there for sometime, 'He's not all bad, you wait until he goes on holiday, you'll soon want him back'. This would puzzle the new arrivals until he did take his holiday, and the whole of the branches' wages would be messed up.

As I mentioned before, Form loved rules; he applied all the rules to his job. This was good as well as bad for the people he worked with, as when Form was on duty, all the time sheets were filled in correctly and in the hands of the wages department with time to spare. So this particular branch of the council held the best reputation for getting wages both correct and on time. Anyone who has worked for any other council department will know that this is unusually rare. He was also spot on about making sure everyone got all their holiday entitlement, and that the wages department were made aware of any promotions or bonuses that were due. An extra task which he took upon himself to implement was to ensure that anyone entitled to benefits, such as disability or lone parent, was made aware of this and he supplied them with all the information and forms they needed.

On the other hand, if anyone took too much sick leave or worse still Form saw them out and about when claiming to be sick, he had no qualms about reporting them. He would also comment on tiny little things such as anyone taking more pens from the store cupboard than he thought necessary. This was the side of Form that everyone hated, even ones who might have liked him otherwise. He had a saying that got up the nose of all the people he worked with, as he would say it about any gripe that they made. 'The rules are there for the benefit of us all, you'd soon miss them if they were gone'. Which is not what people want to hear when in the throes of a good moan.

Nobody seemed to know much about Form though, not that many had really tried to find out. All that was generally known was that he lived alone, had no pets (he often showed disgust about this subject, commenting that 'Animals are not here on earth for the pleasure of humans') was a paid up member of the Conservative Party and his hobby was stamp collecting. The only reason the people at work knew about his hobby was that he had requested that they bring in any foreign stamps for him, which some of them did, and he showed his appreciation and excitement quite verbally. This proved to make his colleagues either say things such as 'Bless him, so easily pleased' or 'Pillock, what a tosser, getting so excited about a couple of crummy stamps' depending on whom or how many people he had upset that day.

He was not without a sense of humour, although he felt that the work place was not somewhere to laugh and joke. He did display this on the works' picnic each year, by wearing a baseball cap that one of the women had brought him back from a holiday in America, which had in large letters on the front 'Form'at' as in Format or Form hat. He found this particularly amusing. Also his Christmas cards were always amusing and individual. If asked, he would perform what he thought was a very amusing version of 'Jake the peg' at the Christmas party, although he did irritate some because he refused to drink any alcohol at all at the Christmas party, as he had to cycle home afterwards and 'Everyone knows people who drink and drive are passive murderers' as he would pointedly say.

I would imagine that most of the people Form worked with imagined him to be the only son of an elderly couple. If they knew the truth about his childhood they would be truly gob-smacked.

Form's full name was Formation of a Beauteous Thing Through Love Johnson.

His mother lived in a hippie commune in the sixties. Form had been introduced to cannabis in the womb, and been able to skin up a joint by the time he was eight. His father had lived in the commune during the summer of '62 and then buggered off, as his mother put it.

After Form's 'natural' birth (only aided by skunk) his mother had decided that all men are bastards and had declared herself a lesbian. Although in later years she admitted she had always been a lesbian but thought she might try out a 'hetro' relationship, and, boy, did she not want to do that again, never mind bloody childbirth, no, definitely not for her.

Form lived in a variety of places that the commune moved to with his mother until he was seventeen.

He lost his virginity at fourteen to one of the other 'children of the commune,' a rather forward and somewhat smelly young girl of fifteen who took it upon herself to tutor Form in the practicalities of sex. Form admitted to rather enjoying these 'lessons' although after a couple of months he dumped the girl for another 'child of the commune' who took more interest in her personal hygiene. Form had a happy childhood although he would not admit that now.

He had a lot of freedom, and most of the people he was surrounded with were happy (even if it was artificially obtained) most of the time. He had little experience of television, everyone in the commune was accepted for who they were, and there was no peer pressure, bullying or possessions.

All the children were well educated in a variety of subjects; Form was held in quite high esteem as he was clearly very intelligent and lapped up his lessons. He did display annoyance at the rather haphazard attitude to the timing or subjects within the schooling. He had tried on occasions to write down some rules for this but no one paid attention to these, declaring that they were exactly the reason they had removed themselves from organized society. The generally held belief in the commune was that rules should be flexible to consider the individual. Form did not agree.

A party had been held in his honour when at last he had to leave the commune to go to university to study law. Everyone in the commune agreed that a lawyer was needed within the commune to stand up for the rights of those who wish to live an alternative life, and to aid them when they protested about the rape of the environment. They wanted Form to tackle the regulations, to promote the idea of flexible ruling. Form wanted to get in there and show them that the rules are for the best. He believed that rules created equality; they believed that rules squashed individualism.

Unfortunately while he was in his third semester at university Form's mother died. It was a truly messy affair; the members of the commune had been making a human barrier in a ditch surrounding their site, when a curious cow had come too close to the edge of the ditch and had slipped in on top of Form's mother, crushing her to death immediately, and injuring two others either side of her.

Form was devastated, and to add insult to injury the local council would not allow her to be burned on a funeral pyre as she wished due to regulations on emissions.

The commune all agreed that Form should carry on with his education as his mother had wished.

But university changed Form.

He joined the debating society. All of a sudden he was privy to the views of students who had been brought up in suburbia, the norm; he began to feel he had been brainwashed with peace and love. He had always known that the chaotic lifestyle of the commune was not ideal, now he saw rights of ownership, the right of society to expect some input from everyone. He saw that the people within the commune had not contributed in the form of taxes, yet they were afforded the protection of the police at times, they made use of NHS facilities, the councils that cleared up after them; he became very disillusioned with their whole attitude.

Then the big one came – AIDS.

The thought that the lifestyle that he had been brought up in was the cause of the spread of this vicious disease gave Form many a sleepless night. The use of condoms had actually been frowned upon within the commune as they avoided using anything that was not biodegradable or recyclable.

Form recalled feeling rather 'square' one time when he had rejected a young man's advances. Gay Rights was a big issue in the commune and he had no prejudice towards gays, but homosexual sex held no appeal for him. Right now he felt angry; more than that, *furious* that the teachings he had been brought up with seemed to be the cause of so much misery for society.

It was then that he decided to become celibate. He did not want to go for an Aids test, but he felt sure he was contaminated. He no longer felt a pride in the lifestyle he had been used to; he was ashamed of it and turned his back on the commune.

He returned to the commune only once, absolutely screaming mad, and raged at them all. Blaming them for all society's wrongs and brainwashing young children into this perverted death wish lifestyle. He told them they had manipulated his ideas about society and rules. The rules are there to protect, not to chain down, and if they were not so fuzzed up with drugs they would see for themselves that God meant sex for the production of children and for no other reason. He collected his stamp collection and left.

Once a free and easy fun loving guy, now a very bitter young man, alone in the world, deciding to live by the rules rigidly from now on.

chapter two

Having a good job and living alone Form led a quite comfortable life. He still retained some of his earlier lifestyle, such as recycling, drinking herb teas, being very aware of pollution and excessive use of the world's resources. But in Form's mind this was what everyone did and was in no way a reflection on the teachings he had been brought up with.

Form had always collected stamps from early childhood when the commune had received letters from their members who were travelling the world. He loved to sit and imagine where the stamps had been, the types of people who had touched them, even imagining the different circumstances and environments the stamps had been made in, and the methods used to get them to their destination. Now however Form's enjoyment of stamps was from a different angle and he loved to work out the mileage a stamp had travelled, the facts about the countries they came from, GNP and population etc. He looked forward with great excitement to the once a month meeting of the local philately society and he was quite a hit with them as many of them had not thought of their collections in the manner that Form did. His interest in another aspect of their hobby expanded their geography no end. On occasions if a person were to turn up at these meetings they could be forgiven for thinking they had walked into a geography A level class instead of a philatelist's meeting.

Form considered the group to be almost his only real friends. He enjoyed going to the pub afterwards with them and would sometimes have one over the eight. He considered this to be OK as he was only walking distance from home and it was always on a Friday night, so he did not have to get up for work in the morning. The conversations always remained around the meetings and never got into heavy subjects that he didn't wish to discuss. They had 'in' jokes and rarely mentioned personal matters. Subjects such as home decorating and food were often discussed and they were all avid watchers of cookery programs, DIY programs and wildlife documentaries. This was Form's social life, once a month, good enough for him, he thought.

Subconsciously Form blamed the actions of the commune members and 'bad' people in general on wild imaginations. He endeavoured to suppress his imagination preferring to stick to reality; he avoided fictional theatre, films or television and music except for the occasional dance at Christmas. Too many people in the 'arts' in his opinion were reckless in their work, not really understanding the harm they did with their warped messages. Although, surprisingly to both himself and others, he did find Billy Connelly very funny if not rather crude. He was sure that Billy's marriage to a psychologist meant he had a deeper understanding of the subjects he spoke about and Form was prepared to accept that Billy was voicing an opinion with which he did not expect everyone to agree.

Over the ten years since leaving the commune and the death of his mother, Form considered he had led a good life. He had completed his legal training but had decided not to pursue it as a career, as he was unsure if the legal profession held the rules in as much reverence as he did; too many 'bad guys' got away as far as he was concerned. His knowledge of the law he felt aided him in implementing the rules at grass roots, where it was most needed and least applied.

He did not often consider himself lonely as he had contact with people on a daily basis and had spent too much of his life living with others surrounding him all the time, babbling on about nonsense and forcing their emotions on him. No, living alone now was pleasant, it suited him fine. He did not want to change a thing. But his destiny was not in his hands, as he would eventually find out.

Form returned home from work in a foul mood. This was unusual as it was Friday night and the meeting of the philately society at 7.30 usually meant he would be in a good mood.

However, today at work, they had decided to celebrate his birthday, which would be on Sunday. When he had returned from his lunch break he had not found his colleagues hard at work as they should have been, but all wearing party hats, blowing squeakers and shouting "Surprise".

Of course he understood that they meant well, but holding impromptu parties in works' time was definitely against the rules. Besides that, how on earth did they expect to meet the deadlines for next week's time sheets if they took time out to lark around?

He was not impressed with the present they had given him either, and no one would admit as to whose idea it had been or who had bought it. An electric nasal hair trimmer!!! Really, thought Form, did they not think he was aware of this? Mother Nature had obviously given him long bushy nasal hair for a reason and he certainly was not going to trim it off, just because some idiotic style guru thought it was unsightly. One of the young girls in the office had photocopied her breasts and made him a card with it. This he thought was a disgusting abuse of work facilities and had told her so in no uncertain terms.

The 'surprise' party was a total failure. All the other office staff had resumed their tasks and the bottles of wine and ready salted crisps had been put away without anyone touching them. The young lady who gave him the card was informed that she should see him on Monday morning when he had given the matter of her behaviour some consideration.

Everyone in the office hated Form with a vengeance and that afternoon, when he got to his bicycle to go home, someone had let down both its tyres and taken his pump. This angered Form but he made a mental note to look at the security tapes on Monday to find out who the culprit was. He had had to push his bike to the nearest garage and use the air hose to inflate his tyres. This had made him late and he had just missed the library where he had hoped to get out a very interesting book about the history of paper making. He had been sure his friends would have been thrilled to learn about how paper had revolutionized the world and led eventually to the invention of stamps.

Yes, today had been a bad day; Form was not happy. He did not even look at his post; no he would leave that until tomorrow when his mood was better. One cannot absorb information properly when one's emotions are high, thought Form. He decided to have a bath, something to eat and go out to the meeting. Perhaps he would be cheered by his friends into dismissing today's disaster for a while.

The evening got worse. On his arrival at the meeting everyone shouted 'surprise' and he was given yet another electric nasal hair trimmer. What is happening to everyone? thought Form, What is this obsession with my nasal hair? He explained his philosophy about his nasal hair, which his friends immediately understood; they apologized for being so thoughtless. But they all wanted to carry on with the party. Form said he had a very interesting talk to give them. Still they wanted to party. "If I don't give this talk tonight it will set the whole agenda for the year off course," he explained. But they still wanted to party. This was not in Form's plans at all. Still this was not work, it was social time, and he could see that he would not have an interested audience if he gave the talk just now. What is the point of giving a talk to people who do not wish to listen? He was sure they would enjoy it much more next month and of course by then he would have got the book from the library. So Form relented and let them have their party, which after some time he did in fact enjoy.

He returned home pleasantly merry, with his electric nasal hair trimmer, (they had kept the receipt and he was going to go into town and exchange it for something he found more appropriate.) As he drifted off to sleep he felt a pang of frustration. He did not understand some people, they just didn't take life seriously enough, or was it he? He must have a chat with God about that one and he had better do it soon. Did God approve of parties? He supposed he did, as far as he could recall, Jesus had gone to quite a few, perhaps he had been too hard on his friends. But parties in work hours, no, that was wrong he knew that deep down in his soul. Yes, playing when you should be working, that was against the rules, everyone knew that. He worked with some very bad people.

Form had a restless night, dreaming of his work colleagues buzzing around the office on huge electric nasal hair trimmers, teeth missing, dirty, and drunk, throwing his files up in the air, shoving their breasts in his face only for them to turn into pencil sharpeners which tried to sharpen his nose.

When Form awoke the next morning he was decidedly flustered by his dreams. Could he be wrong about his nasal hair? Perhaps he should see his doctor and ask his opinion. This might be a symptom of Aids that had not been made public, he could need treatment. He must make a note in his diary to call the surgery on Monday. It was looking like Monday was going to be a busy day. He hoped nothing else would go wrong or his whole schedule would be a shambles.

As Form raised his head from the pillows a pain shot across his eyes, causing him to lower himself back down. He had drunk more than he thought last night. Slowly this time he raised himself up and made his way to the toilet only to discover that his stomach had also been affected by his over indulgence.

Form made himself a cup of valerian tea; that should sort things out. He picked up the post from the hallway and then remembered he had not yet seen yesterday's post. As the day looked promising, weather wise, he took his cup of herbal tea and his post out onto his balcony, a bit of fresh air might brush away his cobwebs. He was annoyed with himself for being so easily led into drinking. If it made him feel like this, it obviously was not worth it. He had told himself this before; in fact he had told himself this not six months ago, really, why did he not listen to his own good advice?

Form always made a point of opening his post in a controlled manner. Firstly he wanted to make sure he did not damage any stamps, secondly he tried where possible to save and reuse the envelopes; thirdly he liked to have time to really read his mail. Sometimes he received letters from members of the philately group whilst on holiday and very occasionally he would get letters from a couple of friends he had made at university. One, David, was an accountant for a large international recording company. Once or twice a year he would go to other offices to do audits and he would usually write to Form when on these trips and enclose the free eye covers they gave you on planes. Form used to always wear them in bed when they shared a house at university. The reason Form wore them then, was that he found the other students were less inclined to wake him up in the middle of the night with a barrage of drunken confessions or just babble when he wore them. He no longer wore them but considered it a nice thought that David always sent him these, it made him smile. David's letters were always amusing. Form did not always approve of David's antics but David did get the job done, he was successful in his work and his work was set in a very social environment. Form supposed that it was a quality required for the job.

The other friend was Kate. She had been sort of seeing Form at the time his mother died. Form had in fact been deeply in love with Kate, but she had been avoiding making their relationship too formal at that time, and his change of attitude and declaration of celibacy had ended any chance of them being anything other than friends. She was a solicitor now, in a small firm in Newcastle. Form did not understand why she still wanted to keep in touch with him; he had treated her badly and he might have given her Aids for all he knew. He had tried on a number of occasions to broach this subject with her but had backed out every time. It plagued his conscience to think that she might be infecting others, not knowing, and it was all his fault. Still he loved to hear from her and replied readily to her letters. She had many problems over the years and always wrote to 'her agony aunt' as she called him, about these. Sometimes Form wondered if Kate had really been his soul mate. Maybe to the other Form, the free and easy one, but not now. He knew sometimes she did not enjoy his return letters, as they of course referred to the rules, and if her problem came via the misuse or bending of any rules, which most people's problems do in some way, he would of course become pedantic about it. The last time she had written to him she had asked him not to lecture her just to be a shoulder. He had replied that if she abided by the rules she would not need a shoulder. He had not heard from her since and that was at least five months ago!

Form settled to read his post. Firstly was a letter from the library telling him the book he had requested about the history of paper was now ready for his collection. Form already knew this as he had phoned to inquire. Next was a special offer on double glazing. Form hated junk mail and his postman knew only too well not to leave any at Form's address. This was however in a normal envelope, so Form reasoned that the postman was not at fault over this. He put the letter to one side; he would write to the firm and tell them firmly that it was an intrusion of his home. If he wanted their products he was more than able to contact them without them pushing their products through his letter box. He had written similar letters many times before.

The next letter was, Form noted, in an envelope of very superior quality. The letter was from a firm of solicitors called, Michael's, Anderton and Downes. Form had never heard of them. His curiosity lit up his face like a beacon. He put the letter down and went into the kitchen to make another cup of valerian tea. He would save that letter until last, much more exciting.

The other letters were both statements, one from his bank which he meticulously checked and the other from the gas board informing him, once again, that his direct debit payments were too high for his account and that he could refrain from making any payments for three months and reduce the following payments by twelve pounds a month. Form would not do this as he dreaded owing money to anyone and preferred to stay well in credit with all things. He had written to them in the past about this and would obviously have to do so again.

Form finished his tea and picked up the solicitor's letter again. It was fine quality paper. He liked that, he rubbed the paper between his fingers and then held it to his cheek, and he smelt it. There is nothing like the smell of good quality paper, he thought.

The letter was short and not very informative. It said: This firm is representing the Stygbee Estate and requests that you attend a meeting of the Estates Directors on Thursday 27th of this month at our offices 2.30pm. Yours etc. etc.

Form was puzzled. What could they want from him? This was indeed very strange. What on earth were they thinking of having a meeting at 2.30 on a Thursday? Didn't they realize he had to work. Mind you, it did seem rather important, maybe he should request a half day holiday. Still, that was leaving it a bit close. He would only be giving them ten days' notice, which he considered to be rather unfair, but then again the rules did say he only had to give two days' notice for a half day, so he thought that would be all right.

Form took out his diary made notes on all the things he needed to do, wrote his two letters and went off to town to exchange that nasal hair trimmer. He had seen some nice herb pots in Argos last time he went to town and decided they would look just fine in his window box on his balcony.

As was his routine on Saturday mornings, Form had breakfast in a small tea room near the bus station. It was the only place in town that did a good selection of herb teas; not that he always drank herb tea but he liked to know that if he wanted to he could. As he sat down to his meal something suddenly occurred to him. The letter from the solicitors had been addressed to Mr F.O.A.B.T.T.L. Johnson.

This was highly unusual as in general he only quoted himself as Form Johnson, even on official business. He was on the electoral register as just Form and with his bank, work; he could not think of anyone who knew his full name. When people asked him about his name he always said it was ancient Celtic. Now he started to worry. Was this going to be something to do with those stupid commune idiots, as he now referred to them? He was going to have to wait twelve days to find out. What if it was them? He would be wasting a half day's holiday. Maybe he should contact the solicitors beforehand, really this was too much. He did wish people would just leave him alone. Another thing to add to his already long list of things to do on Monday; his schedule was really going to be a mess now.

He spent the rest of the weekend arranging his new herb pots, making notes from his library book and rearranging his speech for next month's meeting, and worrying about this blasted letter. He felt sure by the end of the weekend that one of the members from the commune had got into trouble and wanted him to represent them, although this did not make sense as whoever it was, was apparently already being represented. He convinced himself that they were trying to draw him back into their mucky little world. Sleep did not come easily to Form this weekend. Nightmares chased him; he woke three or four times on Saturday night and Sunday was even worse as he also began to worry that he might not remember all the tasks that he had to do on Monday if he was not adequately refreshed.

Monday morning on arrival at work, Form called in the young girl to his 'office' which was really just a sectioned off part of the general office. He was well aware that everyone in the office could hear all that was said. He liked it that way, he felt no need for secrets.

"Chelsea, sit down."

She sat herself down and immediately broke into a frantic apology. "It was only a joke, Mr Johnson, I didn't think it would cause any problems, I'm so sorry, I promise it will never happen again." She looked at him with pleading in her eyes. She had been warned by the others in the office that he would very likely take this seriously, as at first she thought he might forget all about it.

No such luck for poor Chelsea!

"Now Chelsea," said Form, "this office is an integral part of the council. If we do not take our responsibilities seriously many people may suffer."

Chelsea raised her eyebrows. Yeah right, she thought, children would be left maimed in the street because she photocopied her boobs!

Form continued, "I have given this matter serious thought and have come to the conclusion that I have no alternative but to give you a written warning."

"What," said Chelsea jumping up from her chair, "you have to be kidding, this isn't written warning stuff, just a lark, what are you on?"

Form frowned at her,

"Really, just a lark, and was that in your contract when you joined? Chelsea Flowers is allowed to lark about in work time whenever she feels like it. I don't think so. And I don't think that the office was equipped with a photocopier to take pictures of your breasts. Besides anything else, what gave you the impression that I would wish to see your breasts? I know I didn't. All in all, if I refer to the rule book you have violated quite a few regulations. If you are not prepared to accept the written warning I will have no alternative other than to have you dismissed for gross misconduct, which is not being helped by your attitude this morning. I will give you until tea break to consider your situation. In doing so I feel I am being very considerate. Report to me after tea break. That is all, Chelsea, return to your duties."

Chelsea was by now bright red in the face. She looked like she might explode any minute. She walked around the screen; everyone else was staring at the screen as she walked around it. The faces of all the staff were a picture of, disgust, incredulity, anger or resigned acceptance from those who knew Form well.

During her tea break Chelsea went to see the person in charge of personnel and asked for a transfer to another department. She told the whole story and was told to return to the office, accept Form's written warning and that a memo would be sent next week requesting that she move to housing instead. The personnel manager had previous experience of Form and knew only too well what he could be like. He let her know that within this branch of the council itself, Form's written warning would be overlooked if she went for promotion, but he said it would have to go on any official records, and would show up if she wished to go elsewhere.

Chelsea had a bit of a grumble about this, but thought she had done OK out of it all, considering.

When she returned after tea break she was suitably sheepish, and Form felt that she had learnt a lesson in respect for the rules. He was quite pleased with himself for teaching a reckless young lady a good lesson in responsibility. Yet again the rest of the office staff were not talking to Form, yet again he did not notice.

The rest of the day went quite smoothly. He put in his request for a half day's holiday, in duplicate of course. Made an appointment to see his doctor that evening (during his lunch hour and from the pay phone in the canteen). He considered calling the solicitors at the same time but decided that it was probably best if he called from home, more private. He was unsure of how he would react if told it was the commune trying to make contact again.

On the way home he purchased a new bicycle pump and made his way to the doctor's.

He did not mention to the doctor his fear of nasal hair being a symptom of Aids. He just asked the doctor if it could be a sign of something more serious. The doctor informed him that nasal hair was purely a hereditary characteristic and suggested that if it bothered him that much he should get an electric nasal hair trimmer; he understood they were very good!

Form 'hummed and erred' about calling the solicitors when he got home, and eventually he decided that he had had a busy day and would call them tomorrow. Yet again he had a restless night full of nightmares. He awoke in the morning feeling shattered and reprimanded himself for not calling them and putting his mind at rest.

That evening as soon as he returned home, he called them up.

The secretary put him straight through to one of the partners, Mr Anderton.

"Mr Johnson, how kind of you to call so promptly. I know we did not request you to contact us but we were hoping that you would. How can I help you?"

"Well, as you can imagine, I was fairly surprised to receive your letter. It does not give me any information about what exactly you wish to see me about. I would generally like some more details please. I hope it is not bad news."

"Mr Johnson, we have been searching for you for some time now. I am very sorry to say that I do have some bad news for you. I'm afraid your father has died."

Form was shocked. His father, he didn't even know who his father was!

"Mr Anderton, are you sure you have the right person. I never knew my father, I'm not even sure if he knew of my existence."

"Yes, Mr Johnson, we are sure, you are the only person on any records anywhere with the name Formation of a Beauteous Thing Through Love, that is a certainty."

"Mr Anderton, I do not wish to appear rude, this is quite a shock to me, do you mind if I contact you again later when I have had a little more time to digest this? Thank you, goodbye," and Form put down the phone, slumped back in his chair and stared at the ceiling. He was unsure how he felt about this. What a thing to jump at him out of the blue.

Form decided to go down the pub; he felt the desire for a couple of beers and the hustle and bustle of others around him. This needed thinking about for sure.

Another restless night, a very distracted Form all day at work. The staff noticed but chose to ignore it, as they were ignoring Form anyway.

Once again on returning home Form called Mr Anderton.

"Hello, Mr Johnson, I trust you are feeling a little better today?"

"Thank you for asking, but no, could you please answer a few questions."

"Certainly."

"Who was my father, how did he die and why do you want to see me now? Am I in any trouble?" Form's voice grew steadily shrill, as he spoke.

"Now, now, Mr Johnson, calm down, that is quite a few questions. Let me see, firstly, no, you are not in any trouble, far from it. Your father? Well, your father was Joshua Stygbee the owner of a large estate in Norfolk, been in the family for centuries. I am sorry to say that your father had suffered from schizophrenia for many years and three months ago he hung himself. He never married but acknowledged you as his heir some twenty five years ago. We need to see you about your inheritance"

Once again Form was stunned.

"Thank you, Mr Anderton, I will see you next Thursday, bye." And he put down the phone.

Form had barely put down the phone when it rang. This was an unusual sound in Form's house, and made him jump quite visibly.

"Hello," Form said his voice portraying his unease.

"Hello, Mr Johnson, this is Mr Anderton's secretary. He asked me to call you to see if you would require a car to bring you over for your meeting next week?"

Rather indignantly Form replied, "No."

"Will you require directions to find us then?" she replied helpfully.

"No, I am quite aware of where you are"

"All right, Mr Johnson, we will see you next week then. We will be arranging a light tea. Is there anything in particular we should or should not include? I mean is there anything you are allergic to, or you avoid?"

Form felt a pang of guilt for being so abrupt to the secretary.

"Well, I prefer herbal tea and I'm not fond of shell fish, you know like prawn sandwiches, oh! And I don't like anything with cherry in it or marzipan, I, er, I am sorry I was so short with you just then Mrs…"

"Angela," she replied, "no problem, Mr Johnson, any particular herbal tea?"

Form hesitated for a few seconds. "Just chamomile or lavender, thank you, Angela."

"Very well, Mr Johnson, We'll be seeing you next week then, goodbye."

"Goodbye, Angela."

Form sat and stared into space. What on earth was going on? This sort of thing just didn't happen, except in stories. Angela sounded nice, she reminded him of Kate. Kate, his mind turned back and pictured her, a tiny little firecracker, five foot if that, so skinny you thought she might snap, blonde hair in a wild perm, as if it might add to her height, kind, thoughtful, forgiving, with a temper that came from nowhere all of a sudden, never scared to battle with the biggest, a laugh and smile that could light up a room. Perhaps he should give her a call; he must tell someone, and she was the one he wanted to tell. Besides, she was up to date on legal aspects. He had to admit that he was very rusty and had never really been very interested in this side of the legal profession. Yes, advice from a friend, that was what he needed. He would have some dinner and then phone her.

Form was not sure what he expected but he did not expect Kate's answer phone; he did not know she had one. Form left messages on answer phones all the time at work but for some reason he just stammered and stuttered and hung up. That was silly, he reasoned to himself, when Kate hears that message it might worry her, so he phoned back and left her a message saying that it was him who had left that silly message before, and that he had had some very exciting news. "I might need your advice, and I just want to tell someone about it. Perhaps if you're free we can meet this weekend? Phone me back," he paused, "please." He quoted her his number just in case she had forgotten it and hung up.

Form sat by the phone all evening. He watched a gardening programme and a documentary on spiders. He began watching Question Time, but became irritated as it was a discussion on Clause 28, not a subject close to his heart. He was feeling quite buoyant, if he watched that, he knew he would only end up angrily shouting at the television. He did not want to go to bed just yet, it was still quite early, and Kate might still call. So he had a bath and made himself a drink of warm milk. He began to read a book on the American Indians, which he had been meaning to read for a long time. Three chapters and an hour and a half later Form realized he had not taken in anything he had read. It was late now, Kate was not going to ring tonight. Form was aware for the first time in ages of feeling lonely. He had yet another restless night.

Form went to work as usual the next day; he didn't share his news with anyone. His work colleagues were not the people he wanted to tell. He waited again for Kate to call. He contemplated calling her again but he did not want to be pushy. The next day went along much the same; again Kate did not call.

Friday was always the busiest day of the week for Form, and today he was in yet another bad mood. He had received the memo requesting Chelsea's transfer to housing; he suspected it was something to do with her written warning. The memo had been worded to suggest that there was a need for more staff in the housing department, but he knew better! Somehow oil had been spilt all over his parking space and he had to park his bicycle in a public space which he felt was vulnerable. At every opportunity he had checked to see if his bicycle was still there. When he had inquired about the closed circuit television on Monday he had been told it was out of operation and today when he again asked about it they had told him it still had not been fixed. He sent a memo of complaint to the maintenance department. His secretary had smiled to herself as she typed it!

Form picked up the phone on the first ring.

"Mr Johnson speaking."

"Form, hello, it's Kate, sorry for not getting back to you sooner but I've been on a course. I only got back this morning. What's all this good news you've got, sounds exciting?"

Form was flustered, "Oh! Hello, Kate, um, thanks for getting back to me, listen I really shouldn't take personal calls at work, can I call you this evening?"

"Oh! Christ, Form, don't be such a jobsworth. "

"No, Kate, I don't allow the staff to take personal calls and I must set an example. I'll call you this evening."

"Tell you what, Form, I'm coming into town tomorrow. I'll meet you for breakfast. You still going to the usual place?"

Form affirmed he was.

"About ten o'clock then, OK. Bye." And she hung up.

Form looked around the office, had anyone noticed? He felt guilty for the rest of the day, but he was excited about seeing Kate tomorrow.

On the way home from work he stopped into the retail park and bought himself a new shirt and a rather trendy pair of trousers, cargo pants they called them. He tried them on four times throughout the evening, at last deciding to wear them tomorrow.

chapter three

Form had the first good night's sleep in a week that night, dreaming of flowers, great big ones slowly opening to disclose tiny little babies smiling up at him and then softly floating off in the breeze. He felt warm and comfortable, a feeling of peace all around him. He used to have this dream often, years ago; it had always been his favourite one.

The sun was shining when he awoke and Form hopped out of bed with a little skip. He bathed and made an effort to control his hair with some gel that he had in the bathroom cupboard from way back, when he had been invited to a fancy dress party, which he didn't attend in the end. He couldn't remember why now!

He felt himself getting a little too excited so he sat himself down with a lavender tea on the balcony and wondered to himself what Kate would be like now. She might have changed; it was some years since he had last actually seen her. The thought of Kate stirred him, he felt warm inside. This was going to be a great Saturday, he felt sure of that.

As Form walked towards the tea rooms, Kate was already there sitting outside. She looked smaller. The perm had gone! Replaced with, Form guessed, a 'chic' little 'bob' or something, no ragged jeans, instead a feminine floaty dress! Form was surprised at the change that didn't seem to change her at all! She still looked comfortable with herself, confident, assured. As soon as she saw him she jumped up from her seat.

"Form, hi ya, looking good," she drawled with a smile on her face.

"I like the strides, my man, but can I make a suggestion? Untuck your shirt, it'll look much better."

"No," he said, "get off me," wriggling away from her hands that were trying to pull his shirt from his trousers.

She sat back down with a little giggle. Then she leant over and gave him a little peck on the cheek.

"So good to see you, I was going to call you anyway. I was amazed when I got your message, I thought you must have read my mind. I'm down here for an interview. I was hoping I could stay with you this week. What do you think?"

Kate always did this to Form, she bombarded him. He smiled, she hadn't changed as far as he could see; it still puzzled him why she seemed to like him so much after everything that had happened.

"God, it's so good to see you, Kate, you look terrific. When do you intend to start getting old like the rest of us?"

"Never," she replied.

"This is great," said Form. "You're staying for a whole week? That is going to be fantastic. I've got so much to tell you, you won't believe what's been happening to me. Kate I know who my father is!"

"Form, tell me more, how did you find out? Did you look for him? Have you met him yet? Can I meet him?"

"Whoa, slow down, wait a minute, let's get something to eat. I'm starving are you? When did you get here? Have you been waiting long?"

"Good idea, I'm starving too. I got here about 9.15, so not long but I left really early and I wasn't going to eat on the train." She gestured to the waitress inside and they ordered their breakfasts and a couple of large mugs of coffee. Settled themselves down for a good chat.

"Tell me, tell me, I want to know it all."

Form told her about the letter from the solicitors and how puzzled he had been and then he said, "Mr Anderton said his name is Joshua Stygbee."

Kate sat back in her seat. "Form, you're having me on. Joshua Stygbee, but he's dead isn't he, I thought he died a couple of weeks back. You must be mistaken, it can't be him can it?"

Form was puzzled "You know this man?"

"Don't be silly, Form, Joshua Stygbee, Joshua Stygbee, THE Joshua Stygbee, don't be silly you must remember. David used to go on about him all the time, he did his thesis on him. You know, the compact disc man, you can't have forgotten that, how David spouted on and on about how he was going to change the world with these things," she raised her eyebrows and nodded. "He was right too, are you sure you got the name right? He was rather unusual, sounds like the kind of guy that might have been involved with your mother, he'd be about the right age. God Form, this is so exciting."

Form was sitting quite still; his father, a famous inventor! An eccentric millionaire, no, billionaire. Was this real?

"Perhaps someone is playing some kind of joke on me, do you think?"

"Have you got the letter with you? Let me have a look." She perused the letter, "Form," she said quite firmly, "this is real, you really are… we can't wait until Thursday, we'll go and see them on Monday and make sure."

"I can't, I've got work."

"Oh, pish posh to work, this is more important. Hey, are you going to tell David? He'll go mental, I know he will."

"No, Kate I can't just skip off work just like that, it's not right. Any way Thursday's not that far off. I mean I've waited all this time to find out, I'm sure I can wait a bit longer…David, yes, I'll call him."

"Form," she fumed, "you drive me mad sometimes. If this is true you can say goodbye to the bloody council for good."

"Kate, I have to give six weeks' notice before I can leave. I have responsibilities, people rely on me, I can't just run off whenever I feel like it, it wouldn't be right, you know that. Anyway, I don't want to!"

"OK, OK, but phone David now, he might be able to get here by tonight, it would be great, he'll just go crazy. Come on, come on, use my mobile, call him now, I can't wait till you tell him, this is so great."

She grabbed her mobile phone from her bag and pushed it at Form. He smiled and dialled David's number. Kate could hear David's roar as Form told him. She bounced up and down in her seat and clapped her hands like a child.

"Is he coming, is he coming?" she shouted.

"Yes, I am," he shouted back down the phone. "I'll be with you in about two hours, meet you in the Tuckers for a drink at, ahh, let me see 2.30. This is fantastic, see ya in two shakes, kiddo's," and he hung up.

Form was beaming, wonderful things were happening to him and his two best friends were going to be there to share it. Form copied Kate, and jumped up and down in his seat clapping his hands. If anyone from work had seen him they wouldn't have recognised this glowing man.

Kate and Form killed some time looking around town, Kate popped into the library to see if they had any back issues of Hello magazine to show Form, but they didn't. Kate persisted about Form's shirt and he gave in, in the end, and had to agree that after a while it wasn't completely uncomfortable. They talked and talked. Kate asked Form if he had ever considered getting an electric nasal hair trimmer. This time Form laughed a huge hearty laugh, a laugh that he hadn't had for years; he squeezed Kate's shoulders.

"You know I must be mad, I didn't realize how much I've missed you until now."

Kate looked at Form with a suddenly very serious face "I've always known how much I missed you." She blushed and moved away to look in a shop window. Form stood and stared at her, his

39

mouth hanging loose. This is a dream, he said to himself, I hope I don't wake up too soon.

Form hadn't recognised David at all when he walked into the pub. Somehow he had been expecting David to be wearing a suit, probably because he was an accountant, but it was Saturday! He also felt sure that David had always been taller. Anyway, into the pub walked this man, smart casual clothes that sang money, short well cut hair and sunglasses. He immediately recognised Form; Kate was in the ladies.

"Form, what a gas, you guys aren't having me on are you, this fella was my hero. He really was your dad. I've brought a ton of clippings for you to look at, he has, oh, sorry had, the most amazing place. I've been there, I didn't meet him, but he had a studio you know, one of our bands recorded an album there."

"For God's sake, David, say hello first will you. It is the polite thing to do. We haven't seen each other in six years."

"I know, I know but I've been thinking of what to say all the way over here. Where's Kate? By God she can still scream, how come she's here? Are you two an item and didn't tell me? Oh, look there she is, Kate," he shouted.

Kate's face lit up again, and she did a little jump. "David, David, you're here at last, you said you'd be here an hour ago, traffic bad?"

"No, I just spent ages finding all the stuff I could on Joshua Stygbee before I left and I had to cancel a couple of things."

They all sat down together. Form went and got another round of drinks in. Kate and David said as he was now the richest man either of them knew, he would be buying tonight. That might not be strictly true; David new some pretty mega rich folk, but that's besides the point.

The evening seemed to whizz past, they all had so much to say. The main topic of conversation was of course Form's new found wealth, how it was going to change things, what Form's father had done and been like. David knew loads about that. They moved on from the pub to an Indian restaurant, then on to Form's house. Chatting until the small hours of the morning, helped along by considerable amounts of wine. David ended up sleeping in Form's bed. He went into the bedroom to find a photo album and didn't come out. After a while Form went to check on what David was doing only to find him sound asleep on his bed. Form tucked him in and returned to the lounge. Kate agreed it was late and made her way to the spare room, so Form slept on the couch.

It took Form a second or two to realise the sounds he could hear belonged to David. He opened one eye, just a smidge, oh no, sunlight, he closed his eye back again. No doubt about it, Form had a stinker of a hangover. It sounded like David was suffering too; Form could hear his slow heavy footsteps, each one accompanied by a moan or groan. David made his way to the bathroom. Form listened as David had a pee, and then climbed into the shower; he let out a small squeak and a long drawn out groan. Form smiled. It was nice to hear other people in the morning; it was a long time since he had. Form opened his eyes, boy, oh boy, this was a stinker, his head was rotating on its own about three inches above him, he sat still for a while, was he going to be sick... no... maybe... no, no, he was going to be OK. He went into the kitchen and made a pot of valerian tea. Just as he'd finished David came out of the bathroom, shaved, fully dressed (Form couldn't remember David bringing a case, but he was certainly wearing different clothes) but looking decidedly fragile.

"Valerian tea?"

"Oh yes, please, that sounds just the ticket."

"What time is it?"

"Quarter past twelve, not too bad, what time did we go to bed? How come I was in your room? I thought I'd got the couch."

"Too many questions, another cup of tea first, just shut up for a bit, can you?"

"Cold shower helps."

Form made another pot and they went out onto the balcony. They sat in silence for a while, then Form started to laugh.

"You always did manage to get the most comfortable spot, didn't you? Where did you get those clothes from?"

"Habit, I always bring a change, razor and toothbrush. I popped it into the bathroom when I got here. Any sign of Kate yet or is that a silly question?"

"Very."

They sat in the sunshine for a while generally chit chatting about the night's events. After about half an hour Form made yet another pot of tea and decided to take a cup into Kate.

"Kate, Kate, cup of tea," he gently crooned.

Kate just grunted and a hand came out from the lump under the duvet. She pushed it off and sat up. Form was quite flustered to see she was naked; his eyes seemed glued to her breasts for a second. He handed her the cup of herbal tea. Kate took a large gulp.

"Ugh! What is this cack? Form, don't give me your herbal shit. Coffee, hot, black, orange juice, cold, paracetamols, three, now!"

And she slid back beneath the quilt.

"Coffee I have, orange juice I have, paracetamols you're out of luck, I don't have them."

She pulled the pillow over her head and shouted, "Your weird Form Johnson, everyone in the world has paracetamols. I need paracetamols, bugger bugger bum shit bum, just get the coffee and juice will you."

Once they had all sort of returned to normal, Form and David much more so than Kate, they made their way to a local cafe for a cooked breakfast. Kate stopped in at the chemist's and got her beloved paracetamols. Within half an hour they were laughing again.

They returned to Form's house. David grabbed his mobile phone and started checking his messages.

"Form, you got a fax?"

"No"

"PC?"

"No."

"Shit, listen, I've got to pop out again. I've got to get to that cyber cafe in the high street. It's open on Sundays, isn't it?"

Form shrugged.

David made for the door. "Back in about an hour, lunch at The Waterside sound OK? Tell you what, I'll meet you there." And he was gone.

"I thought accounting was a nine to five job," said Form.

"Not in the record business, no job in the record industry is nine to five according to David, it's all go, go, go, pump, pump pump." Kate giggled. "I was really surprised he could come over, I usually have a terrible time just getting him on the phone."

Form realized that Kate and David obviously spoke to each other more often than he thought.

Kate and Form sat waiting for David in the Waterside pub; David was forty-five minutes late. They both began to feel tired, last night was catching up on them.

"What's the interview for?" asked Form

"Women's refuge."

"Doing what?"

"What do you think, der brain, solicitor? I hope I get it, should be a really fulfilling job, better than trying to get a bunch of kids off of ram raiding charges, when you know full well they did it. I'm getting truly sick of it."

"Kate," Form's voice was shocked, "you can't defend clients that you know are guilty."

"Grow up, Form," she said irritably, "I live in the real world. I didn't stay here and hide from life like you did. What are you doing still living here? Christ, you've only moved two doors down from the house we were in, in uni'."

"That place is three streets away, Kate, don't exaggerate, anyway, you know what it was like, we were always complaining to the council about all sorts of things. I thought it best to get in there and sort it out. Things have improved around here, a lot. I'd like to think I had something to do with that."

Kate did not look impressed. "Yeah, well, whatever." She was annoyed with Form, Form was annoyed with Form, he didn't want to upset her. He also knew she could be a moody cow, especially when tired after a night on the piss.

David strolled in and apologized for being late yet again; one could tell he was used to apologising for being late.

"Well, Form, I've done some research, these chaps you're dealing with are *definitely* the right ones, get this, conservative estimate, conservative, mind you, couldn't get near the real info, not yet anyway, are you ready for this?"

Kate butted in, "Get on with it, will you, stop being a wind up, you git."

"OK, but I think it deserves a bit of a build up."

"Come on, tell us," said Kate clearly getting very excited.

"Right, conservative estimate ... two point five Billion Squids."

He jumped up in the air closely followed by Kate, YEAH, YEAH, YEAH, they squealed.

Form sat stunned. He could not take in this sort of information, especially as he had prepared himself to find out all this on Thursday. He looked at Kate and David jumping up and down. He smiled; they looked so happy, he should be happy too, why wasn't he happy?

"David," Form said quietly, "can you get me a drink, a strong one?"

"Champagne," said David with a grand gesture.

"No, I think I'd prefer a good stiff brandy if you don't mind. Get some champagne for you and Kate if you like, but I need a stiff drink, mate. I think I'll throw up if I have anything with bubbles in it."

"Sure thing." David punched Form in the arm and went off to the bar.

Kate calmed down a bit and saw that Form was in shock, not surprising really. She had heard the news as a second party. If it was her who had just received that news she felt sure she would be in shock.

The three of them spent the rest of the day jumping between joy, incomprehension, wonderment, curiosity, a whole gambit of emotions. They laughed a lot and Form shed a few tears later on. Eventually David said he had to leave and would call them on Kate's mobile on Thursday to get the low down.

"Can you come down on Thursday?" asked Form.

"Don't think so, mate," he replied. "I'll try and get some time off as soon as poss'. I'll try for next week, doubt I'll get it, perhaps I'll be sick, eh!"

"NO, you can't do that," stormed Form. Then calmed down. "No, don't do that, just keep in touch on the phone and try to get some time off as soon as you can, OK."

"OK, mate."

With hugs and kisses, pats on the back and punches in the arms, David left.

Form asked Kate if she wouldn't mind if he went to bed; it was early but he had work tomorrow and he felt shattered right down to his bones. He sloped off to bed and who could blame him?

chapter four

The next few days were a roller coaster ride for Form. Kate couldn't believe he was going into work as usual; he wouldn't hand in his notice until he had seen the solicitors on Thursday and he wouldn't budge from that.

All the staff in Form's office noticed that he wasn't acting quite himself, but they were still mad at him over the Chelsea matter.

Kate would insist on phoning Form at work, three or four times a day. Form told her again and again not to, but Kate just pooh-poohed him! Tuesday morning a huge tray of fresh cream cakes arrived at the office and was put into the tea room with a note saying they were from Form. Form didn't know anything about them until he went into the tea room for his break, but he knew Kate had sent them, and he knew her motives were good. But to the staff it looked like Form was trying to butter them up over the Chelsea incident.

Kate went to her interview and breezed it, as Form knew she would. He was very proud of her and told her so about twenty times that evening.

"When do you start?" he asked.

"Two weeks' time."

"How can you start so soon? What about giving your notice at the other firm?"

"Ah! Well, I was coming to that. You see I've already left. I handed in my notice, took two weeks' holiday, went back for a week and then went on that course and that was it."

"Kate, how could you! Hand in your notice, then take your holiday, you must have left them right in the lurch."

"Oh! Pooh to them, they were a bunch of tossers anyway. We're not all like you, Form. I just had to get out, and out of Newcastle as well."

She paused. "I've given up my flat too! All my stuff's in storage. I thought, well you see, I thought, if you didn't mind, I thought perhaps I could stay with you until I find myself a proper place, I mean, no problem if you say no, I can just go into B&B for a while, I just thought, well, you know.."

Form paced up and down for a bit. "Look, no problem you staying, but I am rather annoyed that you did that, you had responsibilities!"

Form continued to whine on about that for quite some time, Kate bit her tongue; she didn't fancy B&B.

David sent a large package to Form's by courier. He had got one of his juniors to research Joshua Stygbee in detail. The parcel had clippings, photos and a brief family history. Form didn't really look at much of the stuff except the photos of his father. He knew now that he had inherited some of his father's looks, especially the hair; in all the photos Joshua too looked as though he was facing into a wind tunnel. Kate greedily read everything David sent and kept trying to tell Form all manner of things, but he didn't want to hear.

"Leave it Kate, I'll do all that in my own time."

She understood and 'left it' but the history of the Stygbee family made fascinating reading.

Kate took Form out to the retail park and helped him to pick out a new suit and some other bits and pieces. She also got him to get his hair cut (not that it made much difference!) She battled with him about not accepting the car to take them to the meeting (Form had already informed them that she would be accompanying him). Form would not budge on that one either. Public transport was fine he kept saying.

"At least take the whole day off on Thursday." she pleaded to no avail.

David sent another courier with a compilation video tape of all the footage his junior could find. Form called his office and left a message saying not to keep sending out couriers, it was much better to post anything, and besides he didn't have a video. The next morning a video recorder arrived by courier! Kate laughed, Form just mumbled his disapproval and refused to watch the tape until after Thursday! However he was talked into getting a video out for Kate and himself to watch on Wednesday evening; she chose Apollo 13, and they got a Chinese take away and a bottle of wine. Form had to admit he enjoyed the evening thoroughly. He went to bed Wednesday night reasonably relaxed.

Form went to work Thursday in his new suit. The morning dragged. Kate was going to meet Form at his office, have some lunch and go on to the solicitors from there with him. Recklessly Form phoned her from his office and told her he would come home at lunch time and they would go from there.

When he returned home Form changed out of his new suit and changed into his cargo pants and a T shirt. Kate was amazed, what was that all about? But Form said it was no big deal, he just wanted to feel more comfortable and not appear too keen. Kate was just a little bit disappointed as Form didn't have any shoes that really went with the cargo pants. Not that he would know that; shoes were shoes to Form.

The solicitors' office was super posh. Right on the top floor of a big tower block, marble and thick carpets everywhere.

Form and Kate were ushered into a very plush office, with a huge conference table with great big leather chairs all around. Form counted the chairs, twenty-four. There was a table laid out with a beautiful buffet and a drinks trolley containing every drink you could think of, plus two stands obviously waiting for champagne buckets.

The large doors at the end of the room opened and about ten gentlemen and two ladies walked in.

A tall smartly dressed fat man came towards Form with his hand outstretched.

"Mr Johnson, pleased to meet you, I'm Anderton." He proceeded to introduce all the others to Form and Kate. Everyone was very polite, even a bit arse licky as Kate later commented.

They all sat down around the table. And so down to business. Form was told that he was the sole heir to the whole Stygbee fortune, which amounted to 3.2 billion pounds excluding property. Investments and royalties brought in a yearly income of 76 million, and there were various trust funds for charities which had to be maintained. Most of the property abroad was allocated for use by charitable organizations providing holidays for a variety of needy people. Although suites for Form's sole use were maintained in all of the properties, boats, planes, helicopters, an island, blah blah blah. Would Form like to go and see the ancestral home?

"What, right now? No, it's too far, I have to be up for work in the morning. I can't afford another late night."

Everyone in the office laughed, except Form and Kate (she knew he meant it, he wasn't joking!)

He was informed he could be there in thirty-five minutes; they had his helicopter on standby on the roof right now. He could go down there and be back by seven or eight if he wanted to!

Kate got very excited at the prospect. Form gave it some consideration and then declined.

"I'll leave it until the weekend if you don't mind, I'll have more time then. I think I need to go home now, thank you all for everything."

"Mr Johnson, surely you want to celebrate, we have some rather fine champagne chilling for you," replied Mr Downes with some concern in his voice. The others showed clear surprise; this was not the reaction they had expected.

"Can I take some home with me?" asked Form. "I'd really like to go home now."

Mr Anderton stuttered, "Well, yes, certainly, we'll get you a car."

"No, thank you," said Form "We bought return tickets, thank you all very much. I'll see you soon, bye," and he walked out carrying a bottle of champagne.

Kate shrugged her shoulders at them all. "I'm sorry about this, it's all been such a shock to him. He needs some time to absorb it all. About the weekend, how do we get there? Never mind, I'll phone you tomorrow and sort that one out, OK, bye," and she followed Form towards the bus stop.

They made the journey home in silence. Form seemed to be on automatic pilot, clutching the champagne to his chest. Kate stared at him with a look of concern on her face, and patted his knee continuously throughout the bus ride.

When they arrived home Form just lay down on the settee. Kate poured him out a glass of champagne and placed a cold flannel on his head.

"Thanks."

She then went down the road and got a pizza. When she returned she knelt down by the coffee table and started to skin up a joint. Form gave her a look of disapproval.

"Leave it out, I was there too, Form."

Form sighed a huge sigh as if he were letting out his last breath.

"Pass it over, will ya."

They spent the next hour in silence drinking champagne and smoking dope. Form didn't eat, Kate polished off two thirds of the pizza and paced up and down, they exchanged smiles every few minutes, but no words seemed to be available to them.

When David called on Kate's mobile she took it into the kitchen and sat at the table.

David was obviously excited and wanted to know everything!

Kate gave him a brief synopsis; David whooped at every bit she told him.

"Listen, David, Form's like a bloody zombie, this is not what I expected, what should I do? I mean he's just in total shock. Should I call a doctor or something?"

"Nah, just be there, imagine how it would be for him if he was alone just now! Give him some time, and talk if he wants too, get him pissed, that should help! Hey! Got any blow? Get him stoned, that'll relax him. Don't worry pet, he'll be OK in a few days."

Form shouted from the lounge, "Tell David to come to the ancestral home for the weekend. I need some advice."

"Did you hear that, David?"

"Yeah."

"Can you make it?"

"No problem, I've already booked it. Tell you what, you get back to Form. I'll call you tomorrow. Bye, pet."

Kate told Form that David would be coming and how excited he was.

Form started to cry! Kate sat by his side with her arm around him, murmuring the usual passive phrases one does when someone starts crying and you don't know what to do.

"I'm worried," Form sobbed. "Look at me, I'm weak, what will this do to me? I've tried so hard to be strong for years. I'm not blaming you but you've been here a week and already I've been getting pissed nearly every night. Now here I am smoking dope. In six months' time I could be right back where I was before I left the commune, throwing away all my principles, not giving a fuck for anything." He paused for a while. "I can't let that happen, will you help me? I know you've got a life," he paused again. "I'm scared to do this on my own."

Kate hugged him tightly. "Form, you need me, I'm there, always have been. Things will work out. It's been a hard day, go to bed now, sleep on it. There's no rush, you can sort things out in your own time."

"Yes, I think I will. Listen, will you sort out about the weekend for me tomorrow. We'll go in the helicopter if you like! Hey, get a helicopter for David as well, will you, tell them we'll be staying the whole weekend, we'll go there tomorrow night. Night, night, thanks for everything, I'm so glad you're here."

Kate put the telly on and gommed out at it for about an hour. She checked on Form and was pleased to see he was sleeping soundly and decided to try and get some sleep herself. It took a while but eventually she got off.

When she awoke the next morning Form had already gone into work. He left her a note saying he would be back by four o'clock because Friday was a short day. Kate took some time to get her act together that morning and was amazed that Form had gone to work at all!

She called the solicitors and spoke to the secretary who said she was at their disposal, and would sort out the car, helicopter and alert the house to their plans. She would also make sure that Mr Stygbee's private secretary was also there for the weekend; he would be able to assist them and introduce them to the staff.

"His name is James Cartwright and he has worked for the family for eight years. He has had to manage the estate almost single handed during his time there because of Mr Stygbee's illness. So he should be a great help," said Angela.

Kate thanked her and called David to let him know the plans. She then called Form at work and got the same telling off as before! Form told her to keep all the news until he got home. She asked if he had handed his notice in; he hadn't. She asked if he had told anyone in the office; he hadn't. She gave up and sat down to wait for his return.

chapter five

Riding in a helicopter is a very exhilarating experience. The ear muffs smother the noise but you can still hear it, and feel the vibration of the propellers. The feeling of speed is amazing and looking down at the sights below gives you a strange perspective.

Form and Kate were like two school children, huddled together, gasping, ohhing and ahhing over the sights they could see. As they approached the estate Form could see a very nice house with Roman columns on the porch and a lovely little gravelled driveway. Some way behind this house he could see a delightful row of cottages which he surmised must be staff accommodation. Not what he thought it would be, very pleasant he thought.

Then the helicopter flew over the trees and into view came a huge mansion. The massive dome on the roof immediately caught his eye. The house he had seen was the gate keeper's cottage, the driveway to the mansion looked to be about half a mile from the gate. The gardens looked beautifully kept with velvet green lawns stretching for what seemed like miles. His heart thumped at the sight of it and he saw a row of people standing in wait for him. He grabbed Kate's hand and held it tightly. He blushed with excitement and worry. He had a feeling that he would make a right fool of himself in front of all these people. What would they expect from him? What on earth was he going to do with all these people around?

As the helicopter landed, two men rushed forward to assist Form and Kate out, and led them towards the line of others waiting to meet them.

A man of about thirty five, Form guessed, very smartly dressed with a fixed grin on his face, came forward and introduced himself as Jamie, Mr Stygbee's personal secretary with an enthusiastic handshake. Form pulled away from him slightly feeling this man was a bit overbearing in his enthusiasm.

The helicopter didn't stop its propellers, so the noise was deafening and Form was straining to hear what was said. After a few minutes the helicopter took off again; it was going to pick up David. Everyone shielded themselves from the wind as it took off and stood still, watching it as it flew off over the trees.

Jamie reintroduced himself and asked Form if he would like to meet the staff as they were all keen to meet the new boss!

Form nervously agreed and was walked down the line: the head butler, Mr Colin Blackwell, his wife the head housekeeper, Mrs Alison Blackwell (Form was pleased that they didn't bow or anything, they just shook his hand), the head groundsman, stablemen. The head cook was a large round woman with a cheery smile and a wide belly laugh. Her name was Mrs Watiniki (better known as Tinny). She was Hawaiian and her husband was Form's main driver. Chambermaids, gardeners, cleaners, drivers, the line seemed to go on and on. Form shyly shook each one's hand, asked their first name and introduced Kate 'his friend' and made a comment to each one that he hoped they would get to know each other better soon. At last the introductions were finished and they were led into the house.

As he walked towards the house Form was aware of the gravel crunching beneath his every footstep and that everyone was staring at him. He felt very uncomfortable and clung on to Kate's hand almost as tightly as he had in the helicopter. He thought back to the helicopter ride and imagined that he must look like a little ant walking up to the massive entrance. He raised his head and took in the imposing front of the house. There seemed to be so many windows, it looked like the entrance to a museum. It didn't look like someone's home, never mind Form's.

As Form entered the vast entrance he expected the place to echo; he was surprised to find that it was all carpeted and felt warm. Straight away one could tell that this house was not the mausoleum Form expected it to be.

They were shown into a huge lounge, resplendent in white, quite modern, flowers beautifully displayed around the room, eight large French doors opening onto the garden, soft sofas and chairs arranged around the room and a table with a handsome buffet laid out. Colin, the head butler, inquired as to their drink requirements and went off to prepare them. Form and Kate both could not help themselves from gawping at the splendour of the room, turning slowly around and around with their mouths wide open.

Colin brought in two glasses of champagne for Jamie and Kate and a pint of bitter for Form on a silver tray and presented them with their drinks. Another gentleman brought in an ice bucket containing two further bottles of champagne and what looked like a wicker wine basket with four bottles of Newcastle brown ale in and left them beside the buffet table.

Alison (the housekeeper) came in and explained that because they were unaware of Form's preferences as far as food was concerned, Tinny thought it best to prepare a buffet with a range of foods, but that she would be more than happy to prepare any alternatives they required.

Form looked at the food for the first time. The table was laid with everything from game pie to tapas to sushi.

"Thank you very much, Alison," said Form, "I'm sure there is something for everyone here, can you tell Mrs... ummm, Tinny, that everything looks great, we have all we need, thank you, thank you all." Form found himself bowing to her like the stereotypical Chinaman.

Alison smiled, "Very well, sir."

"No, no, Form, Form is my name. I'd rather you called me Form." Although Form had always enjoyed the power his position had given him at work, he felt as if he hadn't earned this reverence. He was on their territory, he had done nothing to warrant being called sir.

Alison backed out of the room "I'll try, sir, I mean Form, it may take some getting used to!"

Jamie endeavoured to make small talk and they all perused the buffet table. Kate gulped down her champagne and refilled her glass before attacking the buffet with relish.

"I've never had sushi before," she said as she picked up the bits of raw fish.

Form pulled a disgusted face. There was nothing he could think of that he would be less excited about eating.

As they sat down on the sofas to eat, Jamie said, "I have arranged for two of the team from Chanel to pop over tomorrow, so that they can get you measured up for some outfits."

Kate raised her eyebrows at Form. He smiled and gave a nervous giggle.

"Of course Tatler wants to see you, we hoped for a photo session with them tomorrow afternoon. Sometime over the weekend we need to get together with Mr & Mrs Blackwell and Tinny to organize the party."

"Whoa, whoa," said Form, "you're rushing me a bit here, Tatler, party! These are not on my list of to do's. I think I'd like to take things easy this weekend, just look around the house and grounds, get the feel of the place. I don't want to be in any magazine," he finished with a sigh and turned to Kate for help.

"Can we still see the Chanel people, Form?" queried Kate with a laugh.

Jamie frowned. "You see, there are a lot of very important people who want to meet you. I don't mean to rush you but we have been without a lord of the manor, so to speak, for quite some time. There are many items that need to be addressed, business you understand. The best way to get you into this is really to hold a ball. That way you can get to meet many of the people who are involved in the estate and other interests."

"No," said Form, "I can't do this just yet, leave it for a month or so. What I really want to do this weekend is find out about my father and family. I didn't know anything about them until last Thursday and I want some one to tell me the whole story, I can't just become your lord of the manor in two days. I need time to adjust, I need some answers to some questions. I've met enough people in the last couple of days and I don't want to meet any more. I have names running wild in my head at the moment... I could do with some new clothes though, so we'll see the Chanel people, I can see the sense in that. Do they do shoes? I really need some new shoes. Kate said the ones I've got don't go with anything!"

Jamie tried to object but Form would not be moved. Jamie left the room to cancel some of the appointments he had made for Form.

"He doesn't look too happy with you," said Kate

"I know," said Form, "do you think I'm being a bit stupid about all this? Should I just go along with it all? It's funny, you know, people dream of this happening to them. I never have, it never even occurred to me to want to live this kind of lifestyle. After all I was happy to live in a house that had a toilet that flushed and be able to wear deodorant after I left the commune."

"Form, just remember, you're the boss here, you don't have to do anything you don't want to. Bloody hell, you can afford to hire someone to do just about anything, chill out, let's just ride the ride and see where we end up, eh!"

Form knew she was right. He went over and sat beside her.

"What would I do without you? Give me a hug, it's pretty impressive so far, isn't it though?"

"You bet," she said with her face tucked into his chest giving him a big hug.

"Form," she said in a whinny drawl, "can I have a Chanel outfit too?"

"Kate, you can have a Chanel wardrobe, you can have Chanel toilet paper if you like."

They both looked out through the French doors as they heard the helicopter arriving again. They lightly got up and made their way to the entrance to meet David. David wasn't alone. He had brought three others with him.

"Hope you don't mind, Form, these are mates of mine, Sarah, Louise and Colin. They didn't believe me about you, and I thought we could live it up a bit this weekend. Is that OK with you?"

"Nice to meet you, Sarah, Colin, Louise, no, no problem David, nice to see you, what do you think?" he said throwing his arms out wide to encompass the estate.

"Form, this is totally unreal. I told you, I've been here before, but I only got to see the studio really last time, can't wait to take in the rest of this place. It's not half as stuffy as you'd expect it to be."

Sarah, Louise and Colin, were obviously business people, well set up and used to a good life, but you could tell that this place was well out of their normal dealings. They all dived into the champagne, which Colin (the butler) kept in plentiful supply. Louise harped on about the sushi.

"It's the most in thing at the moment, very trendy."

Form could tell that she was not really his type of person, but with the room filled with people he felt more comfortable and less on display. He was glad David had brought these people along, the house was big enough for him to get away from them if they got too much for him, which he suspected they might after a while.

Later on David asked to be taken on a tour of the house. Form didn't want to go. Alison was nominated to take them on the tour and show them their rooms. Form stayed behind and asked Jamie to go through the family history for him.

"Well, what do you want to know?" he asked.

"As much as you know as far back as you can. From the beginning would be good!"

"It sounds to me as if we should get comfortable. Mr Blackwell, can you bring some brandy into the study? Come with me, Form, I'll show you the way. I think the study will be the best place. Mr Stygbee keeps, sorry, kept a lot of family history in there."

chapter six

"Your family history is a very interesting one. I have most of the relevant details, but I may be a bit rusty on some of the finer points. Really it's a pity your father didn't try to find you when he was well. I'm sure you would rather have heard the story from him."

Form nodded. Jamie poured them both a large brandy and they settled down in the fine leather armchairs either side of the ancient looking fireplace. This room was exactly the type of room that Form had expected to find in a house like this. The walls were crammed with bookshelves, old pictures hung upon the walls, cups and trophies were scattered around in no particular order, busts of people Form did not recognise adorned the mantle and table. There was a smell of tobacco and wood fires that had permeated the room. It was a cosy comfortable room with a feeling that it had tales to tell of its own, of laughter shared sitting in these same chairs.

"I'm sure you are aware there is a history of mental illness in your family, Form. Do you want all the details or do you want me to skim?"

"Tell me all you know, good, bad or indifferent, I want to know it all. David, my friend, could have told me all the stuff that's public, plus a little more, but he never knew my father. That must change things, to have known him, I mean, I'd like to hear what you thought of him."

"Well, I'll give you the background first, what I know of it, later on Mr Blackwell may be able to help you further. Your father had many friends until his illness, I mean he still had those friends but, well, it was different then."

Jamie got up and paced in front of the fireplace for a while and then began to tell the story.

"The Stygbee family were initially farmers. The real fortune began to be amassed when potatoes were introduced to this country by Sir Walter Raleigh, sometime in the 1600s I think. The Stygbee family were the first to grow potatoes in a big way. They cornered the market for decades and made a fortune.

"They were wise and invested very well in all manner of areas. It was then that they built this house. It was designed by your great great oh! I don't know how many greats grandfather Michael Stygbee. He designed it around his other interests, astrology and astronomy. He was involved in building the first real telescope, there is an observatory on the south wing, it's very impressive. Your grandfather made some rather unusual changes to it in the fifties, it really is like no other observatory.

"The original telescope is still here in storage but of course we have a much more up-to-date version now. Science, astrology and astronomy have always been a passion of the Stygbee family. The laboratory in the basement of the south wing excels the most modern in the country. It has always been considered a privilege to study here since the house was built. Just before your father died he had rather a tantrum and kicked out everyone from the south wing. Some of them are very keen to meet you in the hope they may return to their work."

Form gave Jamie a stern look and sighed, "Jamie, I will handle all that in my own time!"

Jamie, slightly disgruntled, continued.

"Yes, well, the history thing, now, this house was the first house in England to have a water purification system and sewerage. The Stygbee's had proper toilets before the royal family you know!"

Form raised his eyebrows and gave a wry smile.

"Inventions and inventors, that's the main source of the Stygbee wealth. You'll be able to look around the laboratory tomorrow. It is a place that has seen the birth of some of today's greatest accomplishments. This house has played host to the world's finest brains."

Jamie got up and walked around the room, searching for a place to start. His eyes lit upon the mantle.

"Here's a bust of William Gilbert, scientist at the court of King James, who came here to study magnetism and electricity." He moved around the room again.

"The reason I said it would be best to talk in here is because this room is like a history book in itself..." he paused again for a while, gathering his thoughts. Form peered around the room with excited eyes, waiting for the next instalment and sipping his brandy.

Jamie took a deep breath.

"Right! Johannes Kepler, considered the founder of modern astronomy, came from Germany to study here for a year.

"Oh! Yes, of course, Torricelli, Galileo's apprentice and inventor of the mercury barometer, see this here," he said pointing to a large barometer on the wall. "This was a gift from him, he stayed here whilst having problems with the church. I'm sure you know enough about history to know all about that."

Form didn't but was not going to show it, and nodded 'knowingly'.

James continued.

"John Napier, logarithms you know.... Descartes, 'I think therefore I am'." James made 'air' quotation marks.

"Sir Francis Bacon, all studied or used the laboratory here at some time. Robert Boyle, thought the father of chemistry and one of the founders along with the Stygbees of the Royal Society for the Improvement of Natural Knowledge, in London.

"Isaac Newton, great friend of the family. We have a file an inch thick of letters from him, totally priceless."

"Really," said Form. "My God, this is amazing, Are the envelopes with them?"

"Some, many of them were sent before envelopes!"

"Do they have stamps on them?"

"Ah! I see what you're getting at. Yes, from its first inception the Royal Mail is logged here. I myself mentioned the value of the stamps some time ago to your father, but he didn't show any interest, the content of the letters was his only interest. All letters remain intact, with stamps. The content of the letters would make any stamp more valuable don't you think?"

"Oh definitely!" Form enthused. "Have they been looked at by a professional philatelist?"

"No, that side of things really was of no interest to your father, or his father for that matter. The idea was to keep a log of scientific data, and also to show the more personal side of the people behind the minds, so to speak."

"I see, I will look at them later, carry on, sorry to interrupt your flow."

"No, that's fine, we can talk about whatever you like."

Form waved his hand at Jamie, indicating him to carry on, although his eyes did wander to the bureau where the letters were kept. He would enjoy looking through that little lot, the other philatelist members would flip when he came up with some of the treasures that must be in there.

James continued.

"Who else? Let me see, Brook Taylor, mathematician, Joseph Priestly, something to do with electrics again!"

James carried on moving around the room, picking up items to assist him with his history lesson.

"The Stygbee family invested in the East India Company as all the big money did. They also invested in the first newspaper. Oh yes! And of course the Pembroke College in Oxford."

He paused and poured another brandy for himself and Form, who was hanging on every word he said.

"This is exhausting, are you hungry? I am. I'll call for Mr Blackwell to get us some sandwiches. Is that all right with you?"

"Do you have to stop now? This is thrilling, I can't believe you're talking about my family. Until now I thought my family's greatest achievement was saving a small wood from being cut down and turned into a car park… I'm sorry, yes, this must be tiring for you, there seems to be so much to tell. I am a bit peckish, can we get some food on the way and then, please carry on."

Jamie called for sandwiches and sat back down.

"Let me see, well, there was some trouble around the time of Oliver Cromwell, I can't recall the details. I believe the family went to Ireland for a time."

The door burst open and in came David, bright faced and obviously under the influence of alcohol.

"Form what are you doing?" he howled loudly. "This house is fantastic, you have to see some of this stuff. Come on, don't be a party pooper, we're all going to the pool, come on, it's fantastic, just bloody fantastic."

Form stood up and helped David to a seat.

"I don't think swimming would be a good idea David, you look too gone to me for that. I'm sure you can find something else to do."

"OK, OK, we won't swim, we'll just go in the jacuzzi. Come on, lap up some of this luxury."

"Where's Kate?" asked Form.

"She's down in the kitchen with the cook and a bunch of your servants, telling them about you." He giggled. "You won't have any secrets when she's finished."

"I haven't got any secrets. Don't call them servants, it makes me sound like some slave trader or something!"

David adopted a prim expression and mimicked holding a handbag.

"Ooo! What's up with you?"

Form scowled at him.

"What am I supposed to call them then? I can't remember all their names, can I!"

"Just call them the staff," Form said abruptly.

Form was slightly peeved at the interruption and it showed in his voice, although he knew there was no point getting stroppy with David when he'd had a drink.

"Listen, David, I've got business to attend to, you know what that's like. Go on down to the jacuzzi and have a party with your friends, I'll join you later. I'm going to take the tour of the house tomorrow when it's daylight and I can get a real feel for it all. Go on, go to your mates and have a good time." He ended on a light note and a smile.

Just then, Colin knocked on the door and entered with a large tray containing sandwiches, another decanter of brandy, a large silver thermos jug (one of those fancy Bodum type things) cups, cream and sugar. The thermos obviously contained coffee.

Form asked Colin to assist his friends, and quietly asked him to make sure they had something to eat to soak up the booze a bit, and to get someone to keep an eye on them if they were by the pool, just to be on the safe side. He apologised for their behaviour. Colin assured him that they were being no trouble.

"We have a recording studio here, Mr Form, and we are quite adept at handling people who may be somewhat boisterous. Don't worry, all will be taken care of. May I say Miss Kate is a very lovely lady, very pleasant company. She has been kind enough to inform us as to some of your preferences, which has been very helpful, Tinny is sending out for some herb teas for you tomorrow."

Form smiled. "Thank you, Colin, I bet Kate didn't call them herb teas!"

Colin discreetly nodded with a twinkle in his eye and removed himself from the room.

They sat back down, Form poured himself a coffee, Jamie had another brandy and took some sandwiches. They sat in silence for a while.

"Colin is very nice. I think I'm going to like him," said Form.

"Most of the serv... umm, staff are nice enough. Some of them have been here all their lives, grandfathers too and all that. Sometimes I think there might be a bit of inbreeding amongst them, they all seem to be related in some way. Still, they are all very loyal. Take Tinny and her husband for instance. They were living in some squalid shack in Hawaii and your father just picked them up and brought them to England! They worshipped the ground he walked on, even when he was ill. I'm only a fairly newcomer, they are still wary of me. I try really hard but I think it'll take another decade before they really trust me. Colin and Alison, Tinny and her husband Romme are very close. I feel sometimes that they have a secret they are keeping from me. Some of his friends prefer to talk to them than myself. It's a bit difficult at times!

Form could see now that his dislike of Jamie had just been down to Jamie's desire to be accepted and make a good impression. He decided that he was probably going to like Jamie too. He relaxed into the armchair, feeling that he could possibly get to feel at home here, which was amazing as he had only been here a few hours and had only seen three rooms in this huge house.

"Now where were we? Do you want me to carry on with the academic side of things? Or do you want to know some of the family stuff?"

"Carry on with the history lesson, please, I was fascinated."

"Yes, well, Ah! Oliver Cromwell, yes, they moved to Ireland for a time, well, not much to say about that really, they set up some farms over there, they came back, and carried on as before." He walked around the room again.

"Ha! Contract bridge, do you play?"

"No, 'fraid not."

"Edmund Hoyle invented that here, not exactly a major influence on the world, but he was a close friend and frequent visitor. Let me see, William Herschel, ever heard of him?"

"Can't say as I have," muttered Form, reluctant to show his ignorance of so many historical events that Jamie seemed so informed about.

"He discovered Uranus, apparently with some homemade telescope in his backyard in Bath. He moved here for many years, and eventually discovered infrared rays!

"The Stygbees helped John Dalton with the publishing of his atomic theory. Not sure if he stayed here but we have a 1st edition and letters from him.

"James Blundell, surgeon at Guy's hospital, developed his technique for the first successful blood transfusion here.

"William Thomson studied here for many years. Of course Hertz took the glory for the discovery of radio waves, but Thompson did all the work here really. He's the man behind the Kelvin temperature scale, you know.

"The vulcanized rubber deal in the mid 1800s brought in a fair amount. The estate invested heavily with Charles Goodyear on that one.

"The family did a display at the Great Exhibition. They didn't seem to be very impressed with it though according to some of the letters. Apparently, quite a few ideas got pinched at that time, along with a few students. Still, that sort of thing happens all the time, doesn't it?"

Form nodded.

"The sponsorship of Charles Leclache, the Eveready battery man, was a bit of a farce. The family lost out on that one. Whoever their lawyers were at the time made a big boo boo.

"Oh! Yeah, get this, John Farquharson, inventor of the single shot rifle, was chucked out from here. They wouldn't have anything to do with guns and stuff like that, lost a fortune with that little moral quirk."

Form interrupted, "Well, I don't think that's really just a little moral quirk, I think it's very noble of them."

"Well, yes, I suppose, speaking of noble, Alfred Nobel wrote tons of letters and tried to come over loads of times but they wouldn't entertain him because of the dynamite and lasting gelatine. Nobel peace prize and all that, bit ironic from the man who invented dynamite."

Form agreed.

"There are so many things it's really hard to get it all out in one go, Form."

"I understand, Jamie, just do your best please."

Jamie slipped into a sing songey voice.

"Letters from Darwin, Alexander Graham Bell, big involvement with Edison of course, invested in Henry Ford, could have made more from that. We've got the first 'Teddy bear' upstairs in the nursery, sent by Morris Mitchton in recognition of the family's work. Should be worth a fortune itself that, but it's as tatty as can be, still, piece of history," he pondered.

"The family missed the money boat many times, like the first electronic data system. We had it here for personal use in the late fifties, used it for research. Ross Perot came along, founded a data processing firm and cleaned up. Still, we were in on the ground floor with microchip, big shares in the Intel Corp. Jack Kilby and Robert Noyce couldn't have done it without the Stygbee laboratory. Gave some assistance to NASA, some sort of coating for satellites. I believe it extends the range or something, exciting, don't you think?"

"Yes, yes, very," Form nodded

"Obviously we got in with Microsoft in a small way, pity we didn't get a bit more involved with that one, then of course in 1978 your father comes up with the compact disc. Didn't make as much as he should have from that but still, as you know, you're comfortable enough financially. There really do seem to be some important experiments incomplete. I have been inundated with requests to return. Some very eminent scientists are chaffing at the bit to get restarted."

Form just looked at Jamie. Jamie felt it best not to pursue this any further at the moment.

"Can we take a break now? It's rather late and I'm shattered, plus a little bit drunk now. I don't think I could do your family story justice right now."

"Thank you, Jamie, this has been wonderful, you go off to bed now. I'll interrogate you about the family stuff tomorrow. Only kidding, it can wait, I've taken in about as much as I can handle for the moment. Thank you very much for this."

They shook hands warmly and Jamie took a wobbly stroll off towards one of the staircases.

Form sat in the armchair, he leaned back and smelt the leather, a smile crept upon his face and then extended into a laugh. He jumped up out of the chair and did a silly jig around the study.

His thoughts turned to Kate, then he realised he had no idea where to look for the others, or for that matter even where his bedroom was. He walked out into the enormous hallway, looked about and tried to work out which way to go. As if from nowhere, Colin appeared.

"Can I help you, Mr Form?"

Form looked at his watch. It was 1.30am.

"Are we keeping you up, Colin?"

"No, sir, I mean Mr Form, sir. I'm afraid it will take me some time to get used to not calling you sir," he fumbled

"Yes, I understand, whatever you feel most comfortable with. I'm a bit lost, Colin, I don't know where my friends are or where I should be sleeping. I rather wanted to see Kate. Do you know where she is?"

"Yes, of course, Mr Form, Miss Kate has retired for the night. She very kindly let us know about your relationship, we had presumed that you would be sharing a room."

Form raised his eyebrows!

"We have put Miss Kate in the next room to yours. Your other friends have all, if not retired, expired!"

"Sorry, I don't get you?"

"Mr David and Miss Sarah are currently sleeping on loungers beside the pool. They are quite comfortable, we have covered them over. We thought it best not to disturb them. Mr Alan is in his room. Miss Louise has expired in the white lounge on the sofa. She again has been covered up and seems to be comfortable."

"Deary me, they sound as if they have been quite a handful, sorry about that, Colin."

"Mr Form, we have not had any visitors here for quite sometime, it is lovely to be back in the swing of things again. Do you want me to show you the way to your room?"

"How long has Kate been in bed?"

"About forty minutes."

"Good, not too long then. I think I'd like to see her before I settle down. Would it be possible to get a bottle of coke and some chocolate, Colin?"

"Certainly, sir, I mean Mr Form, if you would wait here I can get them for you or I could bring them up once I have shown you to Miss Kate's room."

"I'll come with you, get a bit of perspective on this place."

Colin guided Form down to the kitchen, through more rooms than Form had imagined, and then back again to Kate's room. Making sure to point Form's room out along the way and to establish what time they might require breakfast.

Form thought it best (a little suggestion from Colin) that a buffet breakfast be set up in the white lounge from about 9am, as everyone knew where that was and they could wander in when they roused.

They bade each other goodnight and Form tapped lightly on Kate's bedroom door. She didn't hear him so he quietly entered the room.

Form put on the light. The room was massive with a huge bed in the centre of the far wall. Kate was a slight bump in a mass of pillows and quilt. Form tip toed over and crawled onto the bed.

"Kate, Kate" he whispered, "are you awake?"

Kate sat up rubbing her eyes and wiping her mouth.

"Form, all right? How'd it go?" she asked sleepily

"Kate, can I talk to you for a while?"

"'Course, got a drink? I'm parched."

Form held aloft the bottle of coke and chocolate with an air of triumph, slipped his shoes off and climbed into the bed.

"Umm, lovely, just the thing. Can you believe this bed, Form? It's not king-size, it's whole bloody royal family sized. The pillows are ace, I feel like the princess and the pea. So tell me, are you Ok now? You look better. I thought you were going to pass out earlier on. I missed you this evening, I thought it best to let you and James sort things out without my busybodying."

"Thanks Kate, you know, I think this is going to be all right. Sorry, I left you a bit in the lurch, didn't I!"

"Oh! You know me, I amused myself just fine, had to get away from that Louise though. David's lovely, but his taste in people can leave a lot to be desired at times.

"The staff here are just the best. I spent most of the time in the kitchen with Tinny and some of the others. They wanted to know all about you! Don't worry, I didn't tell them anything I shouldn't."

Form shrugged. "Don't think there is anything about me that you shouldn't tell, by the sounds of what I can gather of my family I should imagine they've seen much worse than me."

Form told Kate all that Jamie had told him. She knew most of it already having read all David's stuff and watched the video. She made suitably impressed noises just the same and let him have his glory. They talked well into the early hours and then snuggled down together to sleep.

chapter seven

Form woke early, just after eight o'clock. He crept out of Kate's room and made his way to his own room. It was even bigger than Kate's, quite old in design, but with a very modern bathroom hidden to one side and a walk-in wardrobe, still full of clothes, hundreds of them, shoes, suits, jeans, shirts, ties, pants, socks, everything you could imagine. Form wandered along the rows of clothes, imagining his father in them. His father had obviously been a victim of fashion in his time. Some of the clothes looked awful, even to Form who had no idea about fashion.

Form decided to take a bath and get freshened up. He smiled to himself when he saw an electric nasal hair trimmer in the bathroom; perhaps he might try it out later, if it was good enough for his father, Dad, then it might be OK by him. He then rather nervously, he couldn't work out why, selected an outfit from the wardrobe, just some casual slacks, a shirt, and a pair of shoes. They all fitted perfectly. He stood for sometime in front of the mirror, something he rarely if ever did. He looked just like his father, he had to admit it.

All of a sudden he felt very sad; they might have been good friends if he had known him. It felt so strange feeling the loss of someone you had never even met. In this house however he sensed his father's presence; he would have liked to have known him.

After a while wandering around the house, Form eventually found the white lounge. He hadn't really forgotten about Louise sleeping on the sofa when he had suggested having breakfast in there, it was just that it was the only room in the house that he knew the name of.

Louise was not looking her best it must be said. She was still fast asleep, her head was hanging off the edge of the sofa, her mouth wide open and making slight snoring noises, her hair was a bundle of frizz and her mascara was smudged across her eyes and down her cheeks.

Form thought it best to ignore her for the time being. He went over to the table which was adorned with a variety of delicious food. It took him a while to decide what to have, but he eventually plumped for fresh water melon with big dollops of natural yoghurt and a large glass of apple juice. The French doors at the far end of the room were open and a table and chairs were set out on the patio. Although the weather was a little misty, Form sat outside and took in the view. It was peaceful and quiet, the garden was a beautiful array of flowerbeds and big old sturdy looking trees. Little pathways curved in and out calling you in to wander round. In the distance Form could see the little row of cottages, with washing hanging from the line in the back yard of the end house. He could also just make out what looked to be a children's climbing frame.

This was not what one would expect from a magnificent mansion such as this, there was a real feeling of comfort, homeliness, of family and belonging. He could tell by the way things were laid out that the staff considered the mansion to be an extension of their own homes.

Colin approached Form and asked if there was anything he required, the newspapers would be arriving very soon. Form asked Colin to sit with him.

"Tell me about my Dad, did he ever speak of me? Did you know about my mother? What happened to him? What was he like?"

"Are you sure you want me to tell you these things, Mr Form?"

"Who else is there, Colin? Who else would have known my father as you did? You got on with him, didn't you?"

"Oh! Yes, Mr Form, Mr Joshua was a fine man, I grew up with him. I'm only three years older than he was, we were boys together, when he was smaller he used to follow me everywhere, he was like a little brother to me! I loved him dearly."

"Well then, who better to tell me about him, all of it, good, bad, whatever."

"I have duties, sir, Mr Form."

Form could tell that Colin was a bit reluctant, but he could not think why! Then again this man obviously had a lot of responsibility and Form could identify with that. He more than anyone found a disruption to his plans very disturbing. Colin was the type of person who would have plans and would want to see to the smooth execution of those plans.

"Yes, I understand, perhaps you could delegate to one of the other staff, just for this morning. I'll try not to keep you too long."

Colin agreed, and left to make some arrangements. As he left he passed Jamie coming in.

Jamie looked fresh and vibrant, ready for a day of activity. Form wondered what Jamie had in store for him.

"What a lovely morning," Jamie said. Form wondered if he'd even looked outside.

Jamie glanced at Louise still sprawled on the sofa.

"Someone seems to have enjoyed themselves last night, don't they! I'm ravenous, this brekkie looks wonderful. Tinny as usual has come up trumps."

Jamie helped himself to a full cooked breakfast from the heated trolley and a mug of coffee. Form noted he put four sugars in his coffee. Perhaps Jamie wasn't feeling quite as bright as he appeared, thought Form.

Jamie joined Form on the patio.

"Oh! Not as nice as I thought," he said referring to the weather. "Pity, I'm sure it'll brighten up later. Still lots to do."

Oh no, thought Form, here it comes, what's he got in store for me?

"The Chanel people will be here at noon. So by the time you've had the house tour and some brunch, you'll be ready to see them. The board would like to see you this evening. I've arranged for them to come to dinner at seven, a representative from the science college. Mr Herring can't make it but is sending his secretary and a couple of the charity heads are coming too."

Form gave Jamie a hard stare.

"Listen, Jamie," said Form in a very calm voice, "I know you're trying to please everyone but I told you yesterday, I don't want to do this sort of thing. This weekend is just for me to find my way about. I'm not getting into business stuff. You've all managed quite well apparently without my input, a couple more months won't make any difference.

"The Chanel people are OK, I don't think I need to see them just yet but Kate would like to. My father's wardrobe seems to have all I need in it for now. You'll just have to cancel all the others. Don't book me any other appointments or visitors without asking me first."

Jamie looked very taken aback. "Form, you don't seem to realise, these are very important people."

Form lost it then.

"Look, Jamie, I didn't ask for this, this has all been plonked on me, don't try to bully me coz it won't work. I had a perfectly happy life before and if I want to I will go back to that without a backward glance. So get off my back, give me some time. I haven't even handed in my notice at work. I still have to work out my six weeks' notice. If I take on loads of stuff from here I won't be able to do my job properly. I won't let that happen. So just, just back off."

Form walked off into the garden and followed one of the paths that had been calling him. He was flushed and needed to cool down.

Jamie frantically got onto his mobile phone and started to rearrange things. He could be heard apologising profusely.

Colin met up with Form in the garden.

"I have arranged to be free for the morning. I'm afraid I will be needed after brunch. Is that all right with you, Mr Form?"

"Lovely, lovely."

"Perhaps we could take a stroll to the summer house by the lake. We will have privacy there."

"We have a lake, where?"

"The grounds are very well organized, sir, many things are not in view immediately. The lake is hidden from view of the house by this little copse, although most of the grounds can be seen from the observatory. It has a wonderful view in all directions. It was your father's favourite place."

They strolled along a variety of paths, gravel decking and bark. Form noted the lush grass; it looked like velvet. Each turn in the pathways brought another surprise, a water fountain, a statue, a wondrous floral display.

"How many gardeners do we have here, Colin?"

"Fourteen, Mr Form."

"They do a marvellous job, don't they, or has this been specially done up for my visit?"

"No, the grounds are always like this. It has taken centuries to get it to this stage, of course, but the groundsmen enjoy their jobs, some are very artistic. Mr Joshua encouraged that and gave them a free rein. It's always good to be allowed to take a pride in one's work, don't you think? Too many rules and regulations can sometimes smother insight and initiative."

Form had a think about that one. Surely someone must be in charge and have a plan for a place such as this, free rein, mmmm, not sure, seemed to be working in the garden at least, though!

As they came around the edge of the copse before them stood a quaint white summer house, with a veranda surrounding it and jetty leading to the lake upon which sat two rowing boats and a pedalo.

Colin unlocked the door of the house. Inside it was furnished like a beach hut; there was a variety of wicker chairs and sofas with thick padded seats and also a stack of deck chairs in the corner. A small breakfast type bar at one end and what looked like changing bays at the other. He could see over the tops of the half doors. In each bay there appeared to be a thick white robe hanging up and a shelf with soft fluffy towels. A door led off to what Form presumed would be a toilet (he was right, but it also held some showers and a sauna.)

Colin went over to the breakfast bar and made them both a soft drink; they sat down opposite each other in the wicker chairs.

"Please, just tell me about my father, in your own words, whatever you can think of."

Colin paused to gather himself and began.

"Your father was my best friend, we grew up together. He loved his mother dearly, his father was always rather preoccupied, you see, with the search."

Form was puzzled by this, search, what did that mean? But he let Colin continue uninterrupted.

"Your grandmother died from a most unfortunate accident. Both Joshua and his father blamed themselves for this, their relationship was very difficult after her death.

"You see, they had been sitting around the dinner table and Joshua and his mother were playing, throwing grapes and nuts at each other trying to catch them in their mouths, you know the type of thing. They cajoled your grandfather into joining them, and he threw a nut at his wife which got lodged in her throat. They tried to get it free, really, Mr Form it was awful, they were both slapping her on the back, trying to do that Heimlich manoeuvre, all to no avail. Within minutes she was dead.

"They both took it very badly, they both blamed themselves and each other for it. Sad, sad times for us all.

"Joshua was sixteen at the time. His father was unsure what to do, you see, he had so much work to do, he sent him to boarding school. Until then he had always attended the local school. Joshua hated it.

"Mr Stygbee, with the best intentions, implemented a strict regime for Joshua. When his mother was alive Joshua had always run free to a certain extent, I mean he had all the teaching he should have, both at school and at home, you know, riding, piano, etiquette, tennis, many others, his mother used to include many of us in Joshua's lessons so it did not appear to him that these were chores. Mr Stygbee didn't have quite the same diplomatic skills as his wife, and he and Joshua fought terribly for a time.

"In the later years the search made Mr Stygbee very ill."

Colin looked at Form to see if he understood what he meant by ill. Form nodded.

"I understand, Colin, carry on, please."

"Yes, well, by the time Joshua was twenty, his father would rant and rave at him and restrict him in all manner of things. Mr Joshua wanted to help his father but his father would not trust him with his secrets! Mr Joshua ran away. He told me he had never met anyone like your mother. So liberal, living in the commune was the opposite of being at home. He told no one who he was, he wanted to become one of them. I believe he dabbled with some drugs as well."

"I'm sure he did," said Form.

"He found your mother, I'm sorry, Mr Form, I do not mean to upset you."

"What, no, don't worry, I know what my Mum was like."

"Well, he found your mother, shall we say, in flagrante with another woman."

Form laughed. "Yes, he would have, it's not the way she told it, but it sounds more like the truth."

"Oh! I see, you knew about this?"

"Yes, Colin, my mother was always a lesbian. I had a catalogue of 'Aunties' throughout my childhood. You could say I have lived a life less ordinary than most."

"Well, shall I carry on?"

"Please do."

"Mr Joshua found this very distasteful. He knew your mother was pregnant with his child and dispatched a detective to watch what happened. The detective reported to him every month for about two years. Then he couldn't stand it any more and left. We had terrible trouble trying to find a replacement for him. So in the end we used to go to the commune occasionally as charity officers or some such and distribute blankets and things. Mr Joshua didn't come of course but we reported back to him your progress. He was so proud of you when you went to university."

"Gosh, I remember those visits, it was you then. Great big tins of soup, winter coats, I remember, we used to get so excited when you came. You always had sweets, proper sweets, not home made ones. We thought that was so cool."

Colin smiled. "Yes, that was us, we always enjoyed those trips, you were always such a scamp, always grubby. So were most of the others too, I suppose, but we noticed you more than them, but then you left. We found it hard to keep tabs on you after that. You stopped using your full name, and the people at the commune would not discuss you at all.

"Well, when he returned home Mr Joshua found his father was very ill indeed. They became close for a time, and your grandfather shared his secrets with Joshua. Sadly they had little time together before he took his own life. It is not altogether cut and dried as to whether it was actually suicide. He fell from the observatory; he was apparently perched on top of the telescope and slid off. Personally I cannot think of any reason to be perched on top of the telescope, so!

"Mr Joshua took over his father's search, and as you know, it took him to great heights. The CD business was wonderful, he seemed very happy for a time. Then the illness took hold of him too and you know the rest."

"Did he suffer terribly?"

"No, none of them did really, you see, they heard voices, voices from another planet, these voices inspired them most of the time. The problem only became bad when the voices would want them to do something they couldn't, it's been sort of on-going really. Mr Stygbee was searching for something similar to Mr Joshua's CDs for years and it just cracked him up in the end. Mr Joshua was searching for some vibration thing, but he never found it! But most of the time they were happy, obsessed, but happy. Many of his friends would like to carry on the work, I am sure he would want them to. He banished them just before he died but I don't think he would have wanted them to stop completely. I think he just didn't want them around at the end."

"I wish he'd contacted me before."

"So did he, but when he got ill, he didn't want you to see him like that. He remembered his father and didn't want you to have the same."

"Thank you, Colin, this has been quite an eye opener for me. I think I'll stay here for a bit... alone if you don't mind, I don't want to be rude or anything. I give some consideration to letting those fellas continue their work!"

"Good, I'm glad, Mr Form, I leave you in peace, it's a large chunk to take in. Brunch will be in about forty-five minutes. Do you know your way back to the house or should I send someone for you?"

"I'll manage, thank you again, Colin."

Form went over to the jetty and sat in the pedalo. He felt warm inside, his heart felt cheery! He had never given much thought to his father before all this; his mother had painted rather a black picture of him. But his father had cared for him... his father had been proud of him... his father had watched over him like some guardian angel... those visits, he remembered them well, sweets and cola, nice bread and proper jam. They never seemed to get jam right on the commune, it was always really runny. He recalled an anorak he had been given with a lovely fake fur trim to it; he had worn that until it had fallen apart. All these things, things he remembered with joy. When a person has so little, a slice of bread and jam really can be joy. They all came from his father. Form had never met his father, yet now deep inside he felt loved, loved like he had never been loved before. Form was awash with emotions; he sat and wept, smiling all the time.

chapter eight

As Form neared the French doors to the white lounge he could hear Kate's voice raised in anger.

He warily crept into the room and saw Kate and Louise having a flaming row, almost a cat fight. He looked around and saw David sitting in a chair near the door with his head in his hands. He crept over to David.

"What's happening?" he whispered, not taking his eyes from the two women screaming at each other as they circled a sofa which was covered in bags, hats, shoes and boxes of all shapes and sizes.

Kate if rather red in the face with the veins sticking out from her neck, did look fresh and nicely dressed. Louise on the other hand had obviously not completed any repair work on the damage last night's events had had on her. Her hair was standing to attention, her mascara still smeared down her face and she was only wearing her top and knickers.

"I'm sorry, Form, I should never have brought her here. She's a total pain. Kate came in to find Louise going through all the Chanel stuff and claiming it. Kate went mental, as you can see!"

Kate turned towards David shouting, "David, tell her, will you."

She then blushed, if she could go any redder.

"Form!"

Louise had not noticed Form and continued her tirade.

"This stuff is fair game, he can afford it, a dopey cow like you wouldn't even know where to go in this stuff, you don't wear Chanel to Tesco's you know." She suddenly became aware that everyone was looking at her, ran her hand over her hair and tugged at her top to try and cover herself.

"What?" she shouted. "What are you all staring at me for, she started it."

Form took a step forward. "I think you should go and get yourself cleaned up, Louise, and then you can go home, thank you."

Louise was taken aback.

"How am I supposed to get home? I came here in a bloody helicopter, didn't I!"

David burst in, "Oh! Shut up, Lou, haven't you made enough of an arse of yourself, you really take the biscuit you do. Go and get cleaned up, you look a right state, we'll sort you out a lift home. Alan can go with you, he's an arse too, he got up in the night and pissed over the banisters. Go home, will you, you've embarrassed me enough."

The three friends sat down together and watched Louise as she left the room.

"I can't believe her," said Kate "Where do you find these people, David? She's a right ponce, just a money-grabbing bitch, God, I hate her." She took a deep breath.

"I haven't had a row like that in years." She leaned back in her seat and raised her arms above her head in a stretch.

"Boy, did that feel good, look at me, I'm still shaking."

The conversation carried on, David apologising over and over, Kate pulling Louise apart bit by bit, Form worrying what the staff would think and simultaneously trying to pacify David and calm Kate down.

Eventually a sorry-looking Louise returned along with Sarah and Alan, who also looked rather sorry for himself.

Form called Colin and arranged a lift home for them. Sarah decided to go home with them too, mainly due to Louise badgering her into it. David went out to see them off and try to get Sarah to change her mind. She agreed to come down again the next weekend, just her and David. When he returned he cleared it with Form on the grounds that there were no more unexpected guests just yet.

With all the information he had been given Form felt better, although not all the information had been good. The idea of mental illness did not worry him. He was assured of his own sanity; perhaps the part of him that was his mother was holding away this illness which seemed to have dogged the Stygbee family for so long.

He wanted to explore the house now, but he felt a slight trepidation about the south wing. It was however the south wing that seemed to draw him. The rest of the house he was curious to see, certainly, but the south wing held an intrigue.

Kate was very excited about the arrival of the people from Chanel. Form wanted her to come with him around the house so he decided to wait until she had finished picking out some clothes. In the end both Form and David stayed with Kate and she gave them her own little fashion show. A screen was set up at the end of the room and Kate tried *everything* on. She 'camped' it up, flouncing up and down, twirling and posing, swinging bags and scarves and slanting her hats every which way she could. Form and David cheered and whistled as she waltzed by them only occasionally being serious when they really liked an outfit. Not many of the outfits really fitted Kate. She was much too short for most of them which made them all laugh. In the end the people from Chanel left with a list of outfits to be altered and Kate held on to two evening gowns, a trouser suit, a few handbags, eight pairs of shoes (she was thrilled to own eight pairs of Chanel shoes, she'd never had more than three pairs of shoes at any one time before) and a couple of hats and scarves.

Once the 'show' was finished Alison announced lunch. They sat together and Form regaled all the information to them that he had obtained from Colin. They tossed and turned this about between them, jumping from why didn't he just come and take you home with him, to the scariness of schizophrenia.

David harped on about how he had held Joshua up as an idol, and the impressiveness of the people and discoveries that had turned up in this place. Form told them of Colin's reference to some sort of search, which was not complete. Should he get the students back to finish it? It was probably a good idea, they concluded.

After lunch Form announced his intention to explore. Kate was only too happy to go with him, David asked if he could take one of the horses for a ride to work off the lunch! Form, yet again, was unaware of the horses (he held a slight fear of them, so doubted he would be exercising them) and readily agreed. Colin asked if they would like him to accompany them on the tour. Form asked him to join them in the south wing in an hour or so.

In the beginning of the tour Kate felt sure she knew her way around. She took him to the library, the grand hall, several lounges which varied tremendously in decor, some being in keeping with the house others looking like a picture from Habitat or Ikea. They toured the kitchens and then Kate got lost as they went up a stairway to an area that she had no idea about. Still it was an adventure. They peered into bedroom after bedroom, and tried to work out how many there were but with so many corridors, stairways, nooks and crannies, they gave up on that. Variety seemed to be the theme of the house as no theme threaded itself throughout. The artwork varied from contemporary to modern. As they approached what looked like a large white wall at the end of one corridor they saw that the impression of someone's buttocks were built into the wall. They both found this very amusing and tried to fit their own backsides into the impression. Whoever made the impression was a big person, that's for sure.

They managed to regain their bearings and made their way to the south wing where Colin was waiting for them. He thought it best to start in the basement in the laboratory and work their way up.

"The observatory is best viewed at dusk," he explained. "By the time we have seen the rest it will be the perfect time to see it in all its glory."

The laboratory was everything that Colin had said it was. It took up the whole of the basement of the south wing. It was like a cross between something from a James Bond film and NASA. Two massive wind turbines grabbed your eye immediately, a tank with steps up the side leading to a platform at the top and windows all around the lower level. Peering in through the windows you could see a large fan type thing and loads of pipes and wires inside.

"We drained the water out some years back. They used to use that a lot," said Colin as they walked around the tank.

Computers, machines of all sizes, and cabinets lined the walls which went on for ever, all filled with potions, strange things in jars, tools which one would have to be a scientist to know what to do with. Tables with Bunsen burners, bottles and tubes. A huge tunnel contraption which Colin explained had something to do with velocity. Huge boxes which contained high power magnets; the list went on and on. Form and Kate asked question after question. Colin only had an idea about most. He repeated himself frequently saying science was not his strong point. He had aided Mr Joshua in many experiments, but he was only going through with orders. He had no idea what he was supposed to be looking for! He recommended that Mr Herring might be the man to answer most of the questions.

As they went up to the next floor in the lift they were surprised to find what looked like a works' canteen, which in a way it was. Form noted that the whole area was wheelchair friendly: very thoughtful, perhaps some of the students had been disabled.

"At times we have had twenty or more scientists and students here. They never seem to want to range far from the laboratory so this whole wing is in effect a barracks for them all. The food in general was prepared in the main kitchens and transported here. They had a supply of food to prepare themselves as well as they often ate at irregular times," explained Colin.

The next floor was like a college dorm, lots of small bedrooms and a shower block at the end. None of the rooms were shabby or anything like a real dorm. The emphasis seemed to be to allow as many people as possible to be near to the laboratory. The rooms were very comfortable and stylish, quite a few of them having computers and all of them having a private toilet. The shower block was also luxurious including a steam room and sauna. It's no wonder students wanted to come here really, is it!

As they made their way up to the observatory Form could hear his heart thumping in his chest.

They walked into a huge white marble dome through an archway leading off from the spiral stairway. The roof was enclosed by some kind of metal screen which had constellations printed somehow on them. There were charts of the stars all around the walls giving the whole place a feeling of being a part of space itself.

In the centre stood a telescope unlike anything either of them had seen before. It had a cherry picker to take you up to the observation platform. Wheels and cogs the size of tractor wheels surrounded the platform, which was on a turntable.

Under the telescope was a very comfortable looking sofa, deep and long enough for a tall man to stretch out on, clearly there for meditation and contemplation; a couple of 'rugs' were hanging over the edge. One felt sure this sofa had seen many a scientist sleep through the night.

Colin pushed a large green button at the side of the archway.

The room echoed with loud mechanical shunts, and the roof began to uncover. Within seconds of the roof opening, it was barely open at all, the room was filled with shimmering light. A rainbow of colour filled the whole area.

Form and Kate stood with their mouths agog. Colin beamed; he loved doing this.

"The whole of the roof is made from cut crystal. It turns the whole observatory into a prism. Your grandfather had the whole roof redone in the early fifties, when he began the search. Quite, quite spectacular, don't you agree?"

"I feel like I'm inside a rainbow, in space," said Kate. "This is amazing, I feel washed in colour, no wonder you're so proud of it, Colin, how can you bear to leave it."

"Actually, Miss Kate at certain times it can be too much, midday is awful, can give you a frightful headache. Dusk is the best time, and soon when the sun is gone, well, it is just as you first saw it again!"

Form turned round and around watching the light bounce around the room.

"This is magic, it is pure magic, this is the place to find wizards, fairies, leprechauns, it's enchanting. It feels like a spiritual home, a place to find things you will never find anywhere else. I love it, I just love it, can I get up onto the platform?"

Swathed in reflected light Form and Kate got into the cherry picker and were lifted onto the platform. Standing there twenty feet up, they twirled and turned, hugging each other, heads held high soaking up the experience.

"I feel so light, strange, but wonderful. Full of life, like my batteries have been recharged," exclaimed Form.

Kate stood and watched the colours roaming over her body, stretching her arms and legs to capture the reflections.

Gradually the sun diminished and the colours faded. As the room returned to its previous state, both Form and Kate suddenly felt drained. They sat themselves down on the seats either side of the telescope to catch their breath.

After a few moments they turned to each other and began to laugh, leaning back in the seats and rolling off the emotions they had felt.

"It's like some wonderful sort of therapy, my mind seems wiped of any worries. I just want to do it again and again," said Kate.

"I'm going to have a look through this," said Form gesturing to the telescope. "Just to check out whether anyone is out there pouring some sort of medicine in to the dome. I might just catch them as they leave," he joked, and peered into the lens.

Colin nodded and gave a sort of inward smile.

"Can't see a thing, is this thing turned on?"

"I'm not very good at it, Mr Form, but I'll come up and show you what to do. You need to focus, otherwise you might just be looking at a wall twenty miles away, then all you can see is a hole in a brick! I've done that before!"

Once Colin got the telescope into focus, Kate and Form spent the next hour peering into the sky. Neither of them knew what they were looking at but they had never seen the stars like this before and it was fascinating.

As they returned to ground level Form noticed a large, well sort of like a fire place but bigger, much bigger, in the wall.

"What's that all about, Colin?"

"Humm, well, this is something your great grandfather built on to the observatory. It's sort of like a wind tunnel. Walk inside and look up, you will see the inside is spiralled or swirled. It is in fact a fireplace. The masters often asked for a fire to be lit here. But the grate, look, it's over here on the back edge, is tiny, the fire never seemed to heat the room. I think it was mainly for experiments to do with wind, probably some study to do with the wind and the positions of the stars. They did do some rather strange experiments, sir. Well, you don't make discoveries any other way, do you?"

Colin's speech seemed rather stilted, Form thought. Colin knew more than he was letting on.

Form and Kate peered up into the "chimney." The whole fire place was about ten foot square. The chimney was almost the same and the grate on the wall was more like a small barbecue grate. Very strange. They shrugged. Colin was probably right, some sort of experiment thing. Neither of them being in the slightest scientific, they just accepted that they didn't understand.

"Must have been important to have gone to all the trouble of building this!" said Kate.

"Miss Kate, all the experiments in this house were important, you should see the piles of machines, contraptions, oh! Loads of things that are in storage, all made for vital experiments that went wrong or just didn't work out. Thousands and thousands of pounds spent on trying to prove theories that didn't work. Nothing was too much trouble to build in order to make a new discovery. That's the way it has always been here."

"Well, I may take after my father in many ways, but I'm afraid this science stuff is way beyond me. I have no interest in it at all."

"It will come, it will come," said Colin assuredly and made his way back out of the observatory.

Kate and Form followed him with their eyes, a puzzled expression on both of their faces.

"What was that all about?" asked Kate

"He doesn't know me very well. Perhaps as it's run in the family for so long he thinks I'll get the science bug too!"

"Huh, likely!"

"Yeah, right!"

They made their way back to the white lounge hoping to find David there to tell him of their experience.

Jamie and David were in the study, chatting like old friends. Jamie had joined David for his ride and had tried to pick his brains about Form and to see if David could influence Form to meet with some of the board members and charity officials. David had told him to forget it until Form had given up his job.

"No way will he let any of that slip. He's got this responsibility drive thing going on. He thinks the whole of the council will fall apart if he doesn't, you know, work his full notice and make sure that they have a suitable replacement. Just give up, tell the others they'll have to wait, don't bash yourself about it. When he does take all the stuff on he'll go for it one hundred and ten per cent, mark my words!"

Jamie eased off then and decided to take David's advice. They found they had a lot in common and David lapped up Jamie's enthusiasm for his work, especially when he ran through the famous stars he had met and worked for. David loved to name drop; Kate and Form were never as impressed as he thought they should be!

They all sat around for a while, then David suggested a swim.

"Tell you what, Form, I hope we are dressing for dinner tonight! I've brought my tux and I want to wear it!"

Form turned to Jamie. "Do you think that will be all right, I mean with Tinny?"

"Of course, they can't wait to lay on a big dinner, we could invite…"

He got cut off by Form.

"We won't be inviting anyone, just us four, thank you. Can you sort it out with Alison or whoever deals with this sort of thing?"

Jamie made off to the kitchen area saying he would join them at the pool in a few minutes.

They all larked about in the pool for an hour or so and then made their way back to their rooms to prepare for dinner.

Form found many tuxedos in his father's wardrobe. He decided for a laugh to wear one that had obviously come from the seventies' era. Dark purple crushed velvet with a frilly mauve shirt and purple bow tie. He tried to get the tie right, but in the end he had to ask David to fix it for him.

"I'm not sure Kate will find this funny Form, not if she's done up to the nines in her new Chanel gear."

"Rubbish, she always says I have no taste. How can she deny my exquisite choice? She'll love it," he said sarcastically

The men waited in the hallway and watched as Kate made a dramatic entrance, gliding down the stairway, stopping to pose along the way. David let out a stream of wolf whistles, Form and Jamie called out, "Who is this stunning woman, this goddess?" General comments like that. Kate replied, looking at Form,

"I think I have walked through a time gate. Are we in the seventies? I'm afraid I left my Abba outfit in the bin."

The rest of the evening continued in this light-hearted manner. They all sat around the dining table that could seat thirty people. Form and David at either end, Kate and Jamie opposite each other in the middle. They made a joke of shouting at each other to pass the salt etc. And then all got together at one end of the table for a proper meal.

Tinny had in Form's opinion excelled herself (David reminded him that he had no experience of fine foods in order to have an opinion!)

They enjoyed five courses, including lobster which neither Form nor Kate had ever tried. The sweet impressed Kate immensely as it had edible flowers in it.

They took coffee and brandy in the lounge and then all admitted to being tired and settled off to bed. They had agreed to have a game of tennis in the morning, David was a very competitive chap and warned them they would need to be fresh to keep up with him!

chapter nine

Form woke before the others again on Sunday morning. He crept downstairs and made his way to the study. Along the way he met one of the chambermaids, Christine, and asked her to have some breakfast brought to the study for him.

On entering the study he made straight for the bureau. He had been waiting for this since Friday night. He shuffled through the files eventually finding what he was looking for, the file of letters Jamie had told him about. A hefty file about the size of three or four big box files together, he took it to the desk, his hands shaking slightly with excitement.

He noted that the letters had all been kept in chronological order, very impressive. The beginning letters were not in envelopes as Jamie had said. Some looked to have been rolled into scrolls which had been flattened out, others had been wrapped in paper or cloth. Although Form was tempted to read the letters he could not, he wanted to get to the nitty gritty, the stamps. The first letter he came across with a stamp on almost took his breath away. It was a letter from Charles Goodyear dated 1st May 1840. He sat and marvelled at it. A penny black posted on the first day stamps were introduced. This was the ultimate stamp, boy, was this going to make an impression with the others. He held it tenderly, got out his magnifying glass and examined it. This was for real, this was the real thing. He flushed with excitement. He stood up and announced out loud to himself.

"I own a penny black, I own the first penny black."

He did a little jig and then greedily sat down to go through the rest of the file.

Another chambermaid, Amy, arrived with his breakfast. He wanted to share the good news with someone.

"Do you know what I've got here?" he asked her.

She looked taken aback. "Me, sir, no, sir."

"Oh! Please don't call me that, Amy. Sit down, I'll show you what I've got."

She stood still for a while unsure of what to do.

"Mr Form? You want me to sit with you?"

"Do you know anything about stamps?"

"I'm sorry, Mr Form, do you mean letter stamps?"

"Yes, postage stamps. I have here a penny black sent on the very day that they were first issued. The very first penny black," he said with relish.

She suddenly felt at ease. This man was excited about a stamp he wanted to show her. This house was filled with all types of antiques, sculptures, paintings, this man, her new boss, was like a little school boy excitedly showing off his football cards. He wanted to show her his stamps. She smiled and sat beside him.

She couldn't see the appeal but he was obviously loving it. He marvelled to her about each new stamp he uncovered. She could tell he knew what he was talking about. She felt his enthusiasm spilling over on to her, and found she was getting quite excited too, especially the way he explained where the stamps had come from, knowing when the first one in this country and that country had been produced, telling her how the stamp had changed the size of the world the way the Internet has now. For its time the stamp was a wonder of communications.

Amy sat with Form for the best part of an hour until Alison came looking for her. Form apologized for keeping her from her duties. He thanked Amy for keeping him company. She in turned thanked him and said it was really interesting, she had learnt a lot. Form was very pleased with her response. Another convert to the wonder of philately!

Form heard the others coming down the stairs, mainly because David was loudly making threats as to how well he was going to thrash them all at tennis.

He ran out of the study and met them in the hallway.

"Look at these, look what I've found," he said brandishing some envelopes.

David, Kate and Jamie picked up on his enthusiasm and joined him in his fervent exclamations. They had all heard of the penny black, they knew it was something special. It might not normally have excited them to this degree but Forms excitement was contagious.

Eventually Form was persuaded to allow them to go and have their breakfast and to join them for the game of tennis. Once he was assured by Jamie that he owned the stamps and, yes, he could take them home with him, he was reminded that this place was his home as well.

"Can't quite get used to all this just yet," he commented for approximately the hundredth time that weekend.

The four of them enjoyed an active game of tennis. They played doubles and as one would expect, the vibrant team of David and Jamie totally trashed the uncoordinated Form and Kate. David did a victory dance around the court, and Kate presented him with the winners 'Cup' (which was an empty coke bottle.)

They elected to have lunch in the summer house, after which Form and Kate took a rowing boat out and lazed on the lake. They chatted but not too much and for a while they both dozed off.

Form woke with a start, initially disorientated. He gathered himself and sat watching Kate as she slept.

"Kate."

She opened one eye. "I hope this is important. You just dragged me away from an intimate liaison with Keanu Reeves."

"Keanu Reeves, eh! Listen, I've been thinking, I don't want to do this on my own."

"Whoa, hold up there, Mr. This better not be a proposal!"

"Kate, be serious for a minute. I just thought that you don't have to start at the women's refuge. You can come here with me, sort of like a companion, you know."

Kate sat upright, a look of disdain on her face.

"What would my master want? Perhaps I could read to him in the afternoons and play tunes on the piano for his amusement in the evenings."

"It's not like that. I just think we could spend more time together and enjoy all this," he exclaimed throwing his arms out wide to encompass the surroundings.

Kate calmed a little. "Tell you what, you work your six weeks' notice if you must, and I'll start at the refuge. You can spend a couple of weeks here after you've finished. If you still feel the same, I'll hand my notice in, I only have to work a fortnight's. It gives us both a bit of time. You might find in two weeks that you're sick of the sight of me, and I might find that I love the job. Let's keep our options open, OK."

With that settled they rowed back to the jetty to find David and Jamie sound asleep on the sofa, cuddled up to one another with a half drunk bottle of whiskey in front of them.

The rest of the day passed in a lazy haze. As evening drew in Form asked for the helicopter to be brought to take them home. He thanked all the staff for 'having' him. They gathered their things and left, promising to return the following Friday as before. Form emphasized to both Jamie and David that he didn't want any unexpected visitors. Jamie tried to give Form a mobile phone so he could contact him. Form refused it.

"Contact me at home after work if you have to, otherwise it will have to wait!"

On arrival home Form was surprised how small his house felt; he and Kate both commented on this. Form felt exhausted and made his way to bed by nine, after all, work in the morning!

Form arrived at work on Monday morning as usual, the staff barely acknowledging his existence. Form did not notice as his mind was on other things.

He wrote out his letter of resignation and went to see the personnel officer, who was shocked to say the least. He had to admit that although he had no liking for Form, the man did his job extremely well. He inquired why Form wanted to leave and Form rather grandly explained that he had come into an inheritance and would be taking over his father's estate. He didn't elaborate on this. The discussion moved to his replacement and it was thought best if Form chose a member of the staff to train up as his replacement. The personnel officer shook Form's hand and wished him well.

"I will be working my full six weeks' notice so I still have twenty-two and a half days holiday to come, don't forget!"

Form called for the attention of the office staff and made his announcement. He considered three members of the staff to be qualified to do the job and so nominated them, asking the others to vote for the person they thought best to have as his replacement. He would announce on Friday who had been chosen. Then in a moment of impulsiveness he announced he would be having a leaving party at his new home and would like to invite them all.

The talk in the office, tea room and canteen was of nothing else but Form's leaving. The responses to Form's news of an inheritance was varied. Many disliked Form greatly and begrudged him this; some thought him a pompous idiot and thought that this talk of an inheritance was probably some broken down old house or something; one wise guy cracked that it might be an old post office that he'd got, which would mean he could be surrounded all day with his bloody stamps. Others were quite excited and curious and pumped Form for further information, to no avail. He had six weeks to get through, and he had told them too much already.

The other talk surrounded who would replace him and if they would go to his party or not. Many said they wouldn't, for a variety of reasons. One said it would be full of his stamp geek mates, one said he'd probably have them all lined up to play exciting games such as find the stamp, some said he'd probably be breathalysing them as they left. Quite a few were curious and kept mum about it; they would go along just to be nosy.

Form was quite put out at the fervour his resignation had caused. He badgered them to get on with their work and talk about such things in their own time!

The three people he had nominated to take his place all approached him during the day and sang their own praises in an effort to influence him. One went out at lunchtime and brought everyone in the office a Danish pastry for tea. Form considered that this week would be challenging. In the face of change disruption always occurred. Still the job must be done. He would have to keep on their backs for sure this week!

When Form arrived home Kate almost jumped on him.

"The bloody phone has not stopped all day, they think I'm your bloody secretary or something. Jamie's called about... I don't know, a zillion times, some accountant firm, the solicitors. Oh! Colin called to ask if we needed any help. He's lovely, don't you think, very thoughtful. I couldn't think of anything he could help with, but it was nice of him to call. The heliport called, loads and loads of bloody phone calls, Form, aaarrrgh." She yelled, making a play at pulling her hair out.

"Take no notice of them. Jamie is out of order, I told him to phone me after work if he had to. Well, I'm not talking to him tonight, mind you, I must call Colin. I don't know why but I've invited everyone from work to a leaving party at the house. I'd better let him know so he can sort something out. I think I should lay on transport too, don't you think, don't want any drinking and driving, do we!"

In the end they thought a pub dinner a good option, to get them out of the house and Kate away from the phone. She left her mobile indoors too.

"You'll have to get Jamie to come down here if he's your secretary. I don't know what I'm supposed to be doing."

"Take the phone off the hook if you like, go out shopping or something. Don't worry about it, they'll all just have to wait. I'm not going to be bullied and neither should you."

He told Kate he'd been thinking about the women's refugee and asked her if she thought he should give them his house!

"Wait a bit, Form, I haven't even started work there yet. I don't know what they need. Besides you might think of something else to do with the house. Don't just give it to the first thing that comes to mind."

Of course Kate was right, one minute he wanted to take everything slowly, the next he was rushing in. This party for a start that could be a mistake, still he could also invite the philatelist members, show them the collection.

"Hey, we could get David to find us someone really famous to play at the party!"

There he went again, jumping in. No, that actually sounded like a good idea, he knew nothing about groups or bands or discos or whatever. He called David as soon as he got home.

David promised to look into it and bring some examples of the music.

Form remembered that two of the members of the philatelist group had children.

"Listen Kate, if I'm going to have a party, I could really go to town, have a fun fair for the kids or something. They could stay the night, not the ones from work, no I don't think so, but the others, there's enough rooms."

He smiled. "I've never had a party before, well, not including the ones in the house when we were at uni'. They weren't really my parties, just a load of us hanging out together. I think I might enjoy this."

Kate agreed. It sounded like fun; it couldn't do any harm,

"Go for it, I say."

The rest of the week followed along a similar pattern. At work the talk remained on the subject of Form's leaving and his inheritance and who would take over. The three candidates tried their best to enamour themselves to the others.

On Friday they had a vote, very democratic. Form announced to them all that the winner was Trisha, a thirty-five-year-old single mum, very conscientious and hard working, friendly with most of the others; a popular choice with both Form and the whole office except of course for the other candidates, who glared around the room at their so called mates!

They all wanted to go out for a drink after work, Form declined the invitation as he was keen to get back home and off to the estate.

By seven o'clock they were again whirling over the estate. This time David and Sarah had joined them at the heliport. David was excited about this party. He had a list of names, most of whom Form had never heard of, unsurprisingly. When Form told him he wanted to have a fun fair, David was well impressed.

"Learning how to chill now are we?"

"I could better answer that question if it were asked in English!" said Form sarcastically.

Colin and Alison gave them a warm welcome. Tinny had prepared another exquisite supper for which they all dressed.

Form and Kate found that they quite liked Sarah. They had not been able to get the best impression of her the previous week as she was shadowed by the now infamous Louise.

David sneaked a private word with Form and asked if it would be OK to take Sarah up into the observatory tomorrow afternoon for, nudge nudge, wink, wink.

"It's got to be the most stunning place to do it. Go on be a sport."

"David, I am not your mother. I really don't want to know what you're doing, but if you want some privacy tomorrow afternoon, I'm sure that can be arranged." Form gave him a nudge and smiled. "By the way, don't forget, protection, protection, very important nowadays, David, cover up, OK!"

The weekend passed with Form going to see the horses and taking a carriage ride around the grounds, stopping off to take a look at the staff cottages. There were quite a few children about and Form told them all that they were going to have a big party with a fun fair to which all the children were invited, to a rapturous response.

Saturday evening Form and Kate could not dissuade David and Sarah from waxing lyrical about their truly mystic experience in the observatory.

"It's like making love amongst the stars, thrilling, the best ever." David went on and on about it, Sarah too. Eventually the two star struck lovers departed to, as Form imagined, a rather normal bed to discover each other some more.

In the next few weeks Kate started her job. She found it very interesting and spent most evenings pouring over case files. She explained some of the cases to Form, not always getting the response she expected from him. Quite a few of the cases he considered to be lame, pathetic women who should get off their bums and sort their own lives out. Others he was more sympathetic to. Kate couldn't make him out sometimes.

At work Form trained Trisha in her new job and avoided giving any more of his situation away.

The next meeting of the philately society was a mammoth success. He proudly produced some of the envelopes from the file. He told all his friends there all about his good fortune and invited them to come and stay for the weekend of the party. Many of them looked fit to burst with excitement and they all congratulated him on his good fortune. Talk ran on quite late. Form had to admit rather guiltily that he still had not read the letters which accompanied the stamps. This was met with disbelief; such letters must be thrilling, written by the hands of so many major people. Form promised them that he would allow them to read the letters when they came up. One gentleman looked so excited Form thought he was going to vomit.

Form found that each time he visited the house, he was being drawn more and more often to the observatory. He would just sit in there on the sofa, either with or without the dome being open. He contemplated lighting a fire in the grate a few times but thought it pointless. Sometimes when he dozed off on the sofa, he would wake with a jolt, certain someone had been calling him!

He didn't let this bother him as the observatory was a strange place. Even when awake, everyone knows what tricks the mind can play on you when you are in strange surroundings, although it seemed the more familiar he became with the observatory the more often he would doze and sense being called. He dared not mention it to David or Kate. He knew their response would be to accuse him of seeing ghosts and ghouls.

As the time wore on the preparations for the party got bigger and bigger. Form reluctantly agreed to let Jamie invite some of these VIPs that he had harped on about on the strict instruction that no one was to try and talk business with him *at all* that weekend!

There were now to be two marquees one with a band who would play a variety of different styles and one with a disco and karaoke, the karaoke being Kate's idea. There was to be bouncy castles and fair rides, and they had got a wrestling ring where the players dressed in inflatable sumo wrestler outfits. David was particularly up for that and kept challenging Form to do battle. Transport was to be laid on for everyone; fifty guests including children would be staying the whole weekend.

Form spoke to Colin, Alison, Tinny and other staff members making sure that they were OK about all this work. It was plain to see that this was the sort of thing they did best and loved to do. They were revelling in it. Alison recommended having some children's nurses to maintain crèche facilities to enable the adults to have a comfortable break from the children, and to babysit later at night.

Form could not believe this was going to be his party. He didn't have to do anything much, there was always someone available to sort everything for him. Jamie, Colin and Alison were consummate professionals at this.

The weekend before the party Form took Kate to Paris on a shopping expedition. Kate imagined being flown to Paris in a private jet, but no such luck. Form booked them tickets on Eurostar.

"A much more sensible way to travel," he told her.

Still, they had a wonderful time. They stayed in a nice hotel just a short walk from Montmartre. They had strolls around Pigalle and of course up to the Champs Elysee. They shopped in all the best places, Givenchy, Gucci, Yves St Laurent, Armani.

Form did not buy much, an Armani suit and some shirts, some Gucci shoes. They popped into Calvin Klein and he got some underwear, a couple of T- shirts and a nice jacket. Kate on the other hand got loads of items. She kept querying that it was all right with Form, he loved it,

"Anything you want, darling, daddy's got to keep his love bunny happy now, hasn't he!"

Kate threw him a look to kill with, straightened up and shopped some more.

They had dinner on the Champs Elysee at the Cafe George V and watched the people promenade. They toured around on the Metro and took a trip along the Seine to see Notre Dame.

They held hands a lot during this weekend. Kate kissed Form several times. Form took these as friendly gestures. They lay on the bed in Kate's room laughing at the dubbed television programs. Kate rubbed Form's tired feet and even scrubbed his back in the bath. Kate was giving out signals, but Form's receiver was turned off. Form knew he loved Kate, she knew he loved her too. Somehow Form had managed to turn a potential love into sisterly companionship.

This would have to get sorted, but not just yet. Kate would wait for a better time!

chapter ten

During the week in the run up to Form's party a parcel was delivered to his office while he was out. The parcel had to be signed for so, out of curiosity Sam, one of the office juniors, asked who the parcel had come from. He was told it was some urgent documents from the Stygbee Estate which demanded Mr Johnson's immediate attention.

Well, that was it! The cat was out of the bag. Within hours the whole of the council knew that Form had inherited the Stygbee Estate. Every office buzzed with the news. Suddenly the desire to go to Form's party was overwhelming. Form was encouraged by the last minute response to his open invitation. He had to organize another coach, but it did not concern him. He understood that sometimes people could not confirm arrangements until they had organised other features in their lives. He took the change in attitude toward him as a sign that they had finally realized that he was leaving and wished to show appreciation for his past work.

Kate saw this change differently and said that she thought they had found out somehow. She thought they were in the main a bunch of greedy, nosy, free loading shits. Form thought she was being harsh! He considered that he had been a firm but fair supervisor and would be missed by all concerned.

In the office on his last day Form was presented with a bouquet of flowers, a card signed by everyone and a crystal decanter with the council emblem on it. Form was touched.

As Form, Kate, David and Sarah flew toward the grounds of the house, they thrilled at the sight of the marquees, and fun fair. A hot air balloon was filling up ready to give rides. Lights adorned the trees and exterior of the house, people were running to and fro, and carriages were decorated with garlands awaiting the horses to give trips around the estate; huge flower displays on pedestals were dotted here and there, and a large net containing hundreds of helium balloons of every colour of the rainbow swayed in the breeze; they could see some circus folk preparing themselves, juggling and riding unicycles around the lawn. The helicopter had to land some distance from the house so as not to cause problems. A car waited to take them to the house. Form preferred to walk, listening to the buzz of activity and seeing the lights and sights as he approached the house.

As usual Colin, Alison and Jamie met Form at the entrance. He excitedly assured them that he thought everything was amazing. They in turn informed him of some of the details, times of expected guests etc. Form went to the kitchens to see Tinny and her team. She proudly told him of the planned banquet, which also included having a hot-dog stall, candy floss machines, slush puppy machines, ice cream and toffee apple stands as well as an amazing buffet complete with ice sculptures. He thanked her for her efforts and made off to prepare himself.

In consultation with Kate, Form elected to wear his Armani Suit with a Calvin Klein T-shirt and a pair of loafers, smart, casual, the look he was aiming for. A young lady came and gave Form a shave, manicure, facial and after some discussion he was encouraged to make use of his nasal hair trimmer. The result was impressive and transformed Form into Mr Suave as Kate put it.

Form watched from his window as his friends from the philately society arrived by coach, all taking in the surroundings with awe. He laughed as they all endeavoured to carry their bags, until they were informed the porters would take care of that and show them to their rooms. Children could be heard demanding to go and see the clowns/rides/balloons/food in an excited buzz. As they made their way into the house they stopped and stared at the paintings, sculptures, and chandeliers, gasps of surprise emerging from everyone's lips.

Form listened at the door of his bedroom to the muffled chatter as they passed by. He could hear parents telling children not to touch, murmurs of 'Look at this', 'Look at that'. He heard two people discussing the letters in animated tones, 'And Form has promised to let us read what ever we like!" Once they had been shown their rooms, there were the sounds of doors opening and closing as they checked each others' rooms out, people calling one another from balconies outside, declaring amazement at the size, grandeur, hot air balloon and a variety of different things. Form listened to this banter, not showing his face in case they stopped, a grin on his face that seemed to make his whole body shine.

He could hardly contain himself and felt almost sick with anticipation, Kate tried to give him a brandy to calm him down but Form did not want to drink tonight. He wanted to be in complete control of himself so he would be able to recall everything.

At seven thirty the band and disco started up. Soon after, the other coaches with the council workers arrived. The guests in the house were heard making their way to the lawns. David and Sarah joined Form and Kate in Form's bedroom and watched the party begin to unfold. Form pointed people out to the others, and the little group dissected the party goers for a while. Sarah and Kate were in Form's opinion bitching a bit too much about some of the women's outfits. They all watched with grins at the antics of some of the children, and found it highly hilarious as they saw a child run screaming from a clown offering him a balloon.

Form, Kate, David and Sarah made their way down to join the party. The evening was perfect, not a sign of a cloud anywhere. The breeze was slight, and Form decided that even God wanted this party to be a success.

Acrobats, jugglers, clowns and stilt walkers mingled with the crowd. Balloon animals and hats were made for children and adults alike. Children ran from one thing to another with delighted screams and squeals, candy floss and toffee apples in hand. Waiters almost invisibly ensured that everyone had drinks. People waited for rides in the hot air balloon and carriages, laughing and smiling in anticipation. The music mingled into one lively sound, the band playing a compilation of Beach Boy songs and the disco blaring out Steps and the Spice Girls. Some guests wandered around the exterior of the house and gardens, enthusing at almost everything they saw, enjoying the gardens with their hidden delights.

Form meandered in and out of the crowd, lightly chatting to people as he went, being kissed and congratulated by almost everyone. He refused to be drawn into long conversations, just inquiring if people were enjoying themselves. All who knew Form commented on how well he looked. Form had an added glow and beaming smile, which transformed him from less than attractive to frankly very fanciable, as quite a few of the females from his office commented, some of them with a definite note of regret in their voices. Who would have known what was behind, that nose bush?

He and David did have their sumo wrestling match. The inflatable suits and bouncing floor meant that they stumbled and fell around the ring trying to launch themselves at each other. Rolling on the mat in an effort to get back up again, it was declared a draw as they both found it impossible to stop laughing long enough to hold the other down.

Form took a trip in the balloon. It gave him a view of the house he had not seen before. Going over in the helicopter one found you were travelling too fast to see some things. Form was surprised to see that the chimney in the observatory was not as big as he had thought. Beside the dome it was hardly noticeable. He had also thought that the swirled effect was only on the interior, but he saw that it extended to the exterior as well! He noticed a large shelter of some sort on the roof near the chimney which he had not noticed before and he made a mental note to explore this sometime.

When he returned the party was swinging, the drink had loosened everyone and the dancing and singing had commenced. Kate was giving her rendition of Dancing Queen in the karaoke tent, people were jiving to some rock and roll in the band tent. A young girl about five or six passed Form. He laughingly noticed she had candy floss entangled in her hair and blue lips from one of those slushy drinks; she looked as if she were having a whale of a time. The vast net of balloons was set free. The breeze took them away to cries of delight from the children, some of whom tried to chase the balloons frantically pursued by their parents who brought them back to the main party area.

Jamie of course tried to corner Form to talk to his VIPs, Form allowed himself to be introduced but would not be drawn into long conversation, palming them off with promises of meetings very soon. Some of the VIPs entered into the party spirit with relish, and Form noted that some left soon after meeting him. He would not allow this to spoil his night but he made a mental note of it.

As the night wore on children gradually disappeared into the capable hands of the nursery nurses. A crèche was set up in the conservatory, and exhausted children slept peacefully under the watchful eye of their carers. One or two of the older children stayed until the end, dancing and larking about. At midnight everyone came out onto the lawn to watch an enormous fireworks display set to classical music. They ooo'ed and ahh'ed at the correct times as the sky was lit up for miles around from the display of pyrotechnics and then they noisily returned to the marquees for more partying.

The coaches taking the council workers home was due to leave at 1am but it was almost two before they did eventually go, with shouts of appreciation, wishes of good fortune, groans of nausea and drunken singing. Form was slapped on the back, kissed, had his hair ruffled, pledges of undying affection were laid upon him, declarations of having the best time in their lives, promises to keep in touch. They all eventually clambered aboard the coaches along with balloons, the occasional bottle of champers, one or two flower arrangements and parcels of sweets that Tinny had prepared for the children.

The other revellers who were staying at the house began to wind down, and made their way to bed. Form assisted Sarah in getting a very happy and very affectionate David to bed. He then joined Kate in her room where they sat and discussed the night's events. Form allowed himself a couple of large brandies now. They both felt utterly shattered. The night, they had no doubt, had been a resounding success. They curled up together and slept soundly in each other's arms.

chapter eleven

The next morning was slow to start for almost everyone except the children, who could be heard if one were listening, running up and down the corridors at seven thirty.

The majority of the clearing up had been done by then, and some of the staff occupied the children by enrolling their assistance to burst wayward balloons and take some of the decorations down.

The children were given breakfast on the lawn in the frame of the marquee without its cover; this was thought to be a great wheeze.

When the adults did start to appear, which was not until eleven, the children regaled them with the adventures they had already had, trips on the golf cart used to pack away equipment to the storage sheds, fishing bits of rubbish from the fountains with big nets, visits to the horses, warm biscuits in the kitchen with Tinny. The adults were rather delicate and found it hard to show enthusiasm for such wonders. They were however, very grateful to the staff for keeping their little angels amused and giving them a much needed lie-in.

Breakfast was an ongoing affair in the main dining room until after twelve o'clock. Form engaged his friends into the study for a look at the letters and envelopes that were the most talked about subject at breakfast. Kate, the children, a couple of partners of members of the society and Sarah whisked off to the recording studio, where they made some rather awful tapes, enjoyed by all who partook, playing the drums, keyboards, tubular bells, cymbals, xylophone, bongo's and singing at the top of their voices. All areas were covered from 'Baa baa black sheep' through 'The wheels on the bus' to 'Wannabe' by the Spice Girls and 'Tragedy' Steps style.

The doors around the swimming pool were opened into the garden and a temporary gazebo was erected. The pool was filled with inflatable toys of all shapes and floats in the shape of crocodiles. Kate's group arrived there first; it was by then about three o'clock and appetites were beginning to return. A barbeque was cooking away to one side of the lawn, a variety of titbit's adorned tables scattered about. The children were allowed to have a quick swim before eating only if they promised not to go swimming straight after their food.

Big jugs of interesting cocktails sat on the side, others, similarly interestingly looking, clearly marked for the children stood beside interesting glasses with sparkling things floating apparently inside the glass and wiggly straws attached to the sides. Kate and Sarah made straight for the cocktails, grabbed a steak sandwich each and flopped onto a couple of loungers. They came to the conclusion that kids were just too tiring, passing the responsibility back to the nursery nurses who having had an easy morning were quite happy to take it on.

Just as they thought the others would never reappear, they arrived en masse. Form was searching for David. Sarah informed him David had not yet risen, the last that had been heard from him was a request for a large jug of orange juice and to be left alone!

The talk centred around the letters and stamps. All were suitably impressed; the contents of the letters especially with today's knowledge were cause for both amazement and hilarity. Amongst such enthusiastic company even Kate and Sarah were wrapped up into conversations.

Sarah and Kate both admitted to being quite surprised at how much fun the others were. The idea of the philately society had conjured up images of anoraks and bottle end glasses, buck teeth and bad breath. This just was not so. The rest of the afternoon and evening was spent around the pool, swimming, drinking, eating, laughing and singing. Kate played the tape from the morning recording session. It was met with great laughter, most of the party wanting a copy, it was so bad it was good.

David emerged at seven looking fresh and ready to go. He was met with jeers and jokes, all of which he brushed off with consummate ease. He ate a large plate of barbeque meat, washed it down with a couple of tequila sunrises and became the life of the party. Attempting to cross the pool by running across the crocodile floats, and failing! Challenging one of the children to a Smartie eating contest, and losing! Doing a variety of impressions, most of which involved him diving into the pool and wrestling crocodiles, which no one recognised as Captain Hook, Crocodile Dundee or The Man from Atlantis (this was met with raucous denials that the Man from Atlantis could ever have wrestled a crocodile). David Hasselhoff in Baywatch (same response) and a few others. The whole party ended with some lively dancing and right at the end some soulful songs sung very badly, but no one noticed!

Sunday morning began a lot earlier than Saturday. The guests wanted to have a proper tour of the house and lunch in the summer house was organised. The weather didn't look too hopeful, so Colin had a small marquee set up by the summer house, just in case. The summer house would be too full for comfort otherwise, should it rain during lunch. Form was amazed at how easily any problem could be sorted out by Colin, he never seemed to get ruffled at all. He suggested that the tour should not include the observatory until after lunch at about four o'clock, when it would give a good show. Form agreed it would be a wonderful ending to the weekend.

The tour was most enjoyable and the children added an extra dimension to everything. The wall sculpture of the 'bottom' caused a few laughs, the children found it irresistible and tried to clamber all over it. Returning to the studio once again was a big hit, adults and children alike playing instruments and pretending to be rock stars. David gave them a run down of some of the groups he knew had recorded there, not forgetting to mention that he knew some of them personally. This impressed the children more so than the adults so he elected to talk to them most of the time!

The weather held out for them, lunch in the summer house went very well, a few took to rowing boats for a time, most lazed around, and two porters and the nursery nurses played rounders with the children.

As they made their way back to the house Form tried to describe the observatory to them.

"The first time I saw it was like a mystical experience or something, you feel wrapped in colour, it's very hard to explain. The telescope is colossal, the platform is twenty feet up and that's about twenty feet below the top, maybe more. I can't wait to show you all. Even before the dome opens, it's like being in space."

One little chap harped up, "Are you taking us to space? You're a magic man, you got everything, I want to go to space with you, can I?"

They all found this very funny and the little chap was pleased to have made everyone laugh.

The children inevitably climbed the stairs first, loud squeals were heard and a head popped over the railing to announce, "I was right, he has got space in his house, it's right up here, mum, mum, come and see, space is up here, I'm in space and there's a big rocket here too!"

The reaction from the others was similar to the one Form and Kate first had. As the dome slowly opened and everyone was swathed in colour the room became hushed, they all seemed to soak up the feeling. David whispered to one of the younger men,

"Me and my girlfriend, Sarah, her over there! We did it in here, it was unreal, the best sex I've ever had. Believe me, one experience I'll never forget." At first the young man couldn't believe David was telling him this, and was a bit miffed that David was interfering in his own experience of the dome. Then he considered what David had told him and asked,

"Do you think he would let me and my wife, you know. It must have been.... well, I can imagine but I can't say. It must have been something, I'd love to try it myself."

"Sorry, mate, Form's a bit funny about that sort of thing, you understand!"

Truth be told he didn't understand but he was slightly surprised that he had asked such a thing anyway.

"Show them the chimney, Form," said David.

Form gave David a look which said, 'Shut up and let them enjoy the moment'. He led a couple over to the cherry picker and sent them up to the platform. As soon as he did this the children all wanted to go up, and the peace was shattered. Still they all kept feeling the colours run over their bodies, twirling and turning around, and ignoring the pleas of the children which died down relatively quickly as they too again became immersed in the ambient atmosphere.

Gradually everyone had a turn going on the platform. Form then showed them the fireplace and chimney. They inspected it with interest, and the children wanted to light a fire. David agreed with them and began to put some small twigs that were in a basket by the fireside into the grate.

Colin's usually calm manner changed!

"No, sir, I'm afraid you cannot light the fire, it's just not possible, restricted, errr! Inadvisable."

Form turned to Colin.

"What are you talking about? Let them light the fire, I want to see it too!"

"Mr Form Sir, it really is not advisable, it's, it's it's one of the experiments you know, it would be dangerous with so many people here, especially the children."

"I'm sorry, Colin, but I don't believe that lighting a small fire in this grate is going to harm anyone!"

Colin pulled Form to one side. "I do not understand the science of it, sir, but when the fire is lit, the smoke initially goes up the chimney then it comes down again as sparks, big sparks. They will scare the adults, never mind the children, the sparks are really dangerous! Please don't light the fire, sir."

Form sighed, "This had better be the truth, Colin, It seems unlikely to be dangerous, to me, but I hope it isn't because you haven't had the chimney cleaned or something. I'll take your word, best not to risk anyone's safety."

Form let them know it couldn't be done. Everyone was disappointed but he explained about the sparks and they all agreed that it might be for the best. They returned to the main dome and revelled in its glory a little longer. Then they made their way back to their rooms to pack for their return home.

The children displayed vehemently their desire to stay. Most of the adults shared their reluctance to go.

Form was thanked and thanked again, promises to keep in touch, this time ones he knew were sincere, hugs, kisses and, just to aid the departure, Alison had arranged a present for each of the children to be wrapped and left on the coach. They all climbed aboard quickly to find out what the presents were.

They stood and waved goodbye to their guests and then made their way indoors and sat around in the lounge drinking some cocktails, this time made by David in a rather ham-fisted manner, and with more poke to them. They reflected on the weekend. Form thought he had never been so happy. Never in his life had things gone so right for him. He remembered the scruffy scamp from the commune, running around nicking the adults beers. "I am so pleased I thought to have the children along. It made all the difference, people relax more with children around. They give you pure reactions too, not filtered with jealousy, greed or whatever," he paused. "For a minute there I thought I was going to be quite profound, fell at the post though." He raised a glass to his friends and smiled.

As David, Sarah and Kate also prepared to leave, it struck Form that tonight for the first time he was going to be alone in the house. Well, not alone as such with a staff the size of his, but without his friends, companions. How did he feel about this? Unsure, certainly. Perhaps it would be good for him to spend some time alone here. Besides he was sure that Jamie would be pestering him very soon. So it might be best to make the most of it while he could.

Kate had to go back to work, he knew that, they had made an agreement. He would stick to it, but he knew he would miss her. With so much to do here, next weekend would come round soon enough.

Form took them to the helicopter and waved them off. They said the usual good-byes and professed that they would miss each other and promised phone calls.

Form stood back, a lone figure being blown about by the gusts from the propellers waving to them until he could see them no longer in the distance. He walked slowly back to the house, and stood and looked at it; he would rattle around in this place like a pea in a box.

Form was however very eager to have a word with Colin about the incident in the observatory; he went to hunt him out!

chapter twelve

Form found Colin in the kitchen with some other members of the staff taking a well earned rest.

Colin could sense that Form had something he wanted to say to him and immediately stood up.

"Yes, Mr Form, is there something I can help you with?"

"About the fire upstairs, can you explain properly, please. I don't think you were telling me the whole story"

Colin looked at Alison, Tinny and her husband Romme. They all looked concerned. Form noted this.

"Look, is there something you're all hiding from me. I have a right to know what's going on here, don't think I haven't noticed the comments of the last few weeks, you know, the 'you'll sees' and all that. Do you think we've got a ghost or something? *I want to know what's going on!*" He ended with a bellow which left him red-faced and slightly out of breath.

Form was shaking by the time he had finished. He hadn't realised he felt so emotional about this.

"Mr Form, maybe you should sit down," said Tinny.

The others all sat down around the kitchen table. Form thought they looked like conspirators in crime together. None of them seemed to know where to begin, or if they should be saying anything at all.

Colin leant forward and took Form's hand. Form looked at Colin and his hand and took the pose of a little boy about to be told off.

"We have all been with your family for a long time; there is nothing we don't know about your family, we have shared a lot with them, including secrets, big secrets. We know we need to pass on this secret to you, but it is hard. Your father should have told you, introduced you to it. You might have thought him mad though, most people did. We know he wasn't mad; if we tell you the secret though, you may think we are mad too. It's very difficult for us, we don't know how open-minded you are. Your ancestors were all scientists you see, open-minded, they all had to be."

As Colin spoke, the others all murmured agreement with him. Form just looked more puzzled.

"Colin, what are you babbling on about? If there is something I should know, just tell me!"

They all looked at Colin. Tinny and Alison nodded at him, Romme shrugged his shoulders. Colin took a deep breath.

"It's a bit of a wild story, Mr Form, perhaps you could do me the honour of listening until I've finished and then asking questions or making comment."

"Whatever, Colin, get on with it."

"For the last sixty years your family have all been involved in, well, an experiment, well, making something, or, well, sort of finding something, looking for something. They are helping some, err, sort of people find their relatives so to speak. Most of the inventions that have come out of here in the last sixty years have really come from these, err, these... 'friends.' Everyone has been helping to build a machine. It's very technical, most of the stuff in it had to be invented first. It's taken a long time, it's nearly done, but just the last few bits are not fitting. It drove your father insane. You see the 'friends' are very persistent, he didn't sleep at all for months, and in the end he just wanted to sleep, that's all, I don't think he wanted to die, he just wanted some sleep. The 'friends' know he's gone, they have been waiting for someone else to come and help them. That's you!"

"I'm sorry, Colin, but I'm none the wiser for that lovely speech," said Form in his best 'I'm taking no nonsense from you' voice. "Can you please try and speak in English!"

"Just tell him," said Romme.

"Yes, Colin, just tell me, or perhaps you can tell me Romme?"

"I think Colin should tell you, sir, I don't speak so good as he does, I just does driving sir!"

"Colin?"

They all stared at poor old Colin.

"You're going to think this is crazy, sir, Mr Form, sir!" Colin said reluctantly.

"Just say it, Colin, I already think you're crazy at this moment, so what harm can it do?"

Colin stood up, then sat down again. He was flushed and fidgeted with a napkin in his hand, then he banged on the table and stood up again.

"OK the friends… they're not from here, they're from… you see, they're from another planet!"

All stares turned to Form. What would his reaction be?

"Another planet, another planet, eh! Right, I see, so you're saying that aliens from Mars have been chatting to my relatives for sixty years, fine, just fine, great, in fact…*what are you talking about bloody aliens, how stupid do you think I am?*"

Form took a deep breath.

"Colin, you're a very nice man, so are all of you, *but I'm not a bloody idiot, aliens, aliens **oh! Yeah aliens***… listen, I'm going to bed, I will talk to you all in the morning. Perhaps you can come up with something better by then."

He got up and walked out in a 'don't mess with me' manner.

Colin, Alison, Tinny and Romme all sat around the table looking glum. They discussed between themselves what they should do for quite some time. They kept coming back to the facts as they saw it. Firstly, Form was not ready yet and secondly, Form was not a scientist, will he understand?

Tinny cried a bit, Romme spent most of the time shaking his head declaring that *anyone* would think they were mad. Alison berated Colin for not handling things better. Colin tried to defend himself and kept telling them that Mr Form needed to know. Would they have done a better job?

Form took a bottle of brandy with him to bed and drank most of it in just a few minutes. He sat looking out of his window, muttering to himself about how much of an idiot they must think he was. He pondered for a while the thought that they were trying to send him insane and had done the same to his father.

Aliens, bloody aliens, who ever heard of such a thing? Did they think they were in some sort of bloody sci-fi novel?

He eventually collapsed; the brandy had done its job!

When Form opened his eyes on Monday morning he wished he hadn't. He closed them again. "This has to be about the tenth hangover I've had since finding out about my inheritance. By the time a year is up, my liver will be knackered. I'll be in some hospital with tubes coming out from every orifice, I'll look like Ronnie Wood, this has to stop, no more booze for me, not for a long time. I'll tell Colin not to give me anything but soft drinks, hummmm, Colin, I think I'll just pretend what they said last night was drink talking.

"They didn't have anything to drink, did they? Maybe they were just pulling my leg, just to test me out. These old houses are usually full of ghost stories, it's just a new slant on that old theme. If Colin were Scottish and looked more like Private Fraser from Dad's Army... 'We're doomed, Captain Mainwaring,' he probably would have pulled it off better! Yeah, that had to be it, they're probably laughing their heads off at me."

Form rolled over. On the side table was a tray holding croissants and jam, melon and yoghurt, a thermos with valerian tea and some orange juice. They really are very good at their job he thought, and poured himself a tea. He noticed a little note on the tray.

Mr James is here to see you at your convenience, it said.

He doesn't waste much time, well, I'm not going to rush myself. I think I'll be sick if I do. I'll finish this pot of tea first, then I'll try the cold shower thing, or perhaps a warm bath might be better!

An hour later Form met Jamie in the study.

"Please be gentle with me, Jamie, I'm a bit delicate this morning. I want to get down to some business but let's take it one step at a time, OK!"

"One step at a time, got the message. So where do you want to start? I have a list of your charity involvements, accounts for the main estate, requests for the laboratories, staffing, investments, take your pick!"

"Ugh! Really so much?"

"'Fraid so, I need to gen you up on almost everything. That's if you want to be involved in all of it. I mean you can be as involved as you like. Best to find out what there is first though, don't you think?"

"Yes, yes, listen, there are a few things I want to set rolling straight away. I noticed that there isn't a public swimming pool for miles. Let's build one for the school and village, a big one, with all those slides and stuff, OK!"

"Where do you want the pool?"

"How close to the village does the estate go?"

"The village is on the estate!"

"Oh! Right, well close to the village, nearest big field I suppose, just check out the possibles and we'll make a decision later. Oh! And while we're at it, if they do have a scout pack thing, we should set up the lake for them to do canoeing or something on it. Find out what they want or need, would you mind?"

"No, of course not, anything else?" said Jamie furiously scribbling in his massive filofax.

"Look, I've got all this money, what are the chances of me spending it all and getting into debt?"

"Nil, listen, Form, you have seventy-five million pounds a year coming in as a certainty. This will go up, it won't go down, that's for sure, so unless you can spend one and a half million a week you're not even going to touch it really. Shall I give you a run down?"

"Just a general idea, please, nothing too complicated. I'm good with figures but not this morning. These amounts sound, well… unreal, I need some perspective."

"Right, this house is an asset, it is worth eight and a half million. It costs at most one and three quarter million to run, that's when we have a full house in the south wing. This includes the running of cars and horses. On top of that your father spent one and a half million on equipment and supplies for the laboratory in the year before his death. Some years he spent a lot more. The helicopter, boat and plane cost around two million a year between them. Last year that was cut by two thirds because they were hardly used. The other properties add a further twenty-two million with running costs again at about one million. The island is worth fourteen million and as yet has no speakable running costs. Your father's charitable donations in the last year came to just over fifteen million. So you see even with expenses you're still left with about fifty mil a year to play with."

"What about taxes and insurances, stuff like that?"

"All the amounts we are dealing with are net amounts, after tax. Insurances, well, yes, you do pay just over two million in different insurances. Believe me, Form, you're safe to spend, there are no hidden bills or surprises, it's all wrapped up very nicely. The Stygbees may have had some shifty advisors in the past but their accountants have always been top notch. No one will be able to take this away from you, not unless as I say, you manage to spend, say, two million a week for the next ten years or so! Think you can manage that?"

"Really, sounds like monopoly money to me, two million a week! No, I can't see me managing that. What have I spent so far?"

"What, personally spent?"

Form nodded.

"Well, the party came to about twenty-eight thousand, you've spent about ten grand on clothes. I'm not completely sure but over the last six weeks you've spent less than fifty grand, peanuts really."

"OK, I feel better now, I thought I'd spent loads. Well, I have, fifty grand eh!... right, down to business, let's get the south wing back on track. Who was here before?"

"Mr Herring, some of his crew, Mr Bagley, was making frequent trips over. I think we had approximately twelve here."

"Right, well, invite them to return if they wish."

They carried on talking about details. Form gave all the staff a rise, against Jamie's advice. He booked to see all the charity board members the following week. He asked Jamie to organise a holiday for him and Kate to Mexico where one of his villas was situated. Jamie was told to give Form's old house to the women's refuge as soon as Kate was ready to move out. Form called David and asked him to speak to the accountants on his behalf and come back with an explanation of it all that Form could understand. "In real English, please," he asked. He also informed David that the studio was back in use if needed by any artists. Form had hardly put the phone down from David when Jamie received a call on his mobile from David's firm wanting to book the studio for the following week.

"Who... who do they want it for?" whispered Form.

Jamie covered the mouthpiece. "Someone called Supergrass! Do you know them?"

"No, never mind, let them come anyway, it might be company. Will they be staying?"

"Looks like about two weeks, is that OK?"

Form nodded and went to another room to phone Kate. He apologised for phoning her at work, but did she know of a band called Supergrass? She certainly did and seemed very excited; could she bring some friends down when they were there. She shouted to the others in the office, and Form could hear screams of delight. It looked like he was going to have another houseful sooner than he thought!

Colin announced lunch. Form turned to him with a grin on his face. He tapped his forehead, "Ha! You really had me going last night, Colin. Aliens, ha! Yes, good one, I fell for that one!"

Colin looked slightly disappointed. "Yes, Mr Form, we had you going there, didn't we! I understand Mr Herring and Mr Bagley are to return. I must say I'm very pleased. I'm sure you'll enjoy their company."

"Well, science isn't really my thing, but they are welcome to carry on with their work. We have a famous band coming too. I don't know them but Kate is very excited."

"Wonderful, sir, do you recall their name?"

"Supergrass."

"Oh! Yes, a lovely bunch of chaps, very nice indeed, Tinny was very fond of them, lots of midnight snacks. If I recall, her avocado salad was a big favourite of theirs!"

Form did enjoy his lunch even with Jamie constantly on his mobile phone throughout. Four students were coming down the next day and Jamie informed him that Mr Herring would be down on Thursday.

"Jamie," inquired Form, "am I supposed to know this Mr Herring and the others. Everyone says their names as if I should know who they are!"

"Well yes! Mr Herring is a very famous scientist, Professor Herring, Samuel Herring, you know, writer of 'Who put that Black Hole there?!' Surely you've heard of him. You must have seen him on the telly. He did some adverts for BT."

"Oh! God, him!… The genius fella with the voice box, him, really, he wants to come here?… Bagley!… You're not talking about the clockwork radio man are you?"

"Yes."

"That was a brilliant idea. He's coming here too?… I can't speak to these people, I'm no genius… what will I say?… God, Jamie what have you got me into? Tell them I can't see them, just settle them in and tell them to get on with whatever they're doing, tell them I can't, I can't… tell them I'm too busy."

"They're very nice, they don't bite, they do speak about normal stuff too, you know. Please meet them, just for dinner on Thursday, just to welcome them. Then you can leave them to it if you want."

"I don't even know who these people are! I'm a science ignoramus… I'll talk to Kate, see what she says. Don't book anything about dinner until I get back to you!"

chapter thirteen

Kate made Form feel like a right idiot when he told her of his concerns about meeting the scientists. She said he suffered from intelligentism (her word for discriminating against people because they are intelligent - or more so than you!)

She assured him that they would not be talking about electromagnetism and stuff like that.

"They'll probably be more interested to find out if you'll carry on with your father's work and carry on funding them! That's what they'll want to know about for sure. You are going to let them carry on, aren't you?"

"Well, yes, of course I am, I just don't want to look a complete twat, that's all, I just feel a bit out of my depth. I can't possibly spend all this money. These blokes know what they're doing, I'll just throw money at them and hope they do a good job of whatever!... by the way, fancy Mexico in couple of weeks time?"

"For how long?"

"As long as you like."

"Form, my job! Can we talk this out at the weekend? I'll check out if I can take any holiday. I've only been here a little while, it might be dodgy."

Form understood perfectly. He also understood how frustrating it must have been for everyone else when he refused to give up work without working his notice. He and Kate had made a deal. Two weeks of him on his own, then if they both agreed she would give up the job and move in. He'd only been in the house one day and already he wanted her here all the time. He missed her too much.

Form found himself once more in the observatory, lying on the couch. His thoughts wandered to what Colin had said the night before! Perhaps they were so loyal to his father that they chose to believe him in his insanity! To build an observatory like this, space must have been an obsession. It was easy to imagine that with all this surrounding them, when such a terrible disease as schizophrenia hit them, they would imagine the voices were from space.

At night the observatory was chilling. It seemed to be even more a part of space than during the day. He had the screens open and stared into the night sky. The crystal ceiling almost magnified the sky making it surround you. He understood the attraction of such a place to a man like Professor Herring. Did the Professor think his father was insane? He had not read anything of the professor's work, and he did not know anything about his theories. Was he one of those who believed in extraterrestrial life? Was he as kooky as his father had been? He'd better meet him, the whole world seemed to think he was a genius. He'd sort of like to know what a man like this thought of his father.

He drifted off to sleep, the peaceful surroundings lulled him away. He dreamt of being lifted, lightly, like being suspended on a cloud, as you see angels floating away in films. He felt he was being called again, softly. They weren't calling his name, they whispered "Contact, contact," over and over again. Gradually Form stirred, he felt old and confused. He looked towards the chimney. Perhaps he should light the fire if he came up here again at night, it was quite old. He still felt in a dream-like state and made his way to his bedroom, undressing as he crossed the bedroom floor, and crawled into bed like an exhausted child.

chapter fourteen

By the time Thursday had arrived Form was looking forward to meeting Professor Herring. He had met the students who all seemed amiable enough, if a little scruffy. One, Tom, seemed to be totally scatty, often getting lost in the house and having to make several trips backward and forward as he forgot what it was that he had come for! Form always found people like this very annoying, and he could not understand everyone else's attitude to Tom. They found him humorous and delighted in his chaos. Tom took all their leg pulling in good humour and often agreed with them. But to Form's annoyance he made no attempt to improve his behaviour.

Their arrival had been a busy affair, and not at all what Form had thought it would be. They arrived in two trucks with long trailers and began unloading crates as soon as they arrived. The staff all seemed prepared for this and efficiently managed the removal of all the items to the south wing with ease. The students seemed to know a lot of the staff by name, and much back slapping and handshaking went on. Form observed from his bedroom balcony; he felt very shy, sort of voyeuristic as well; he didn't want to meet them but he was drawn to watch them. He reminded himself frequently that this was his house, but he still felt like a nosy neighbour. As they came toward the end of their unloading Form forced himself out to meet them and welcome them to his house. They were, as Colin and Jamie had said, very nice, and overjoyed to be returning. They all thanked him profusely.

Professor Herring arrived an hour early for dinner. Form had not expected this; he was not dressed for dinner, and had only just got out the bath. He felt like a naughty schoolboy caught with his trousers down when Colin announced the professor's arrival. Form fluffed and flustered trying to get dressed as quickly as possible. He stumbled down the stairs and arrived in the lounge fully out of breath and unable to speak.

Professor Herring made Form almost immediately at ease, and made a joke about Form being almost as unintelligible as he was. He thanked Form for restarting the programme, and soon began to speak of Joshua, telling humorous anecdotes of their times together. The staff knew Samuel's (as he insisted on being called. Form could understand the staff's problems with calling him sir as he could not stop himself calling Samuel professor) eating regime and dinner passed as a very pleasant affair. Samuel explained that he had other commitments but he would like to stay for two days and return later if that was all right with Form.

He then asked Form if they could have a chat together in the study! It sounded serious to Form. He was not sure he wanted to hear whatever Samuel had to say. He felt unable to deny Samuel's request, and they sat themselves opposite each other by the fireplace.

"I have a journal of your father's, I was trying to collate all the information from it into a book. Your father asked me to do this. The journal has rather a lot of personal notes which were not to be included. I think your father would like you to read it. Your grandfather also had a journal. Some of it is missing but I also have what is left of that. I have spoken to Colin and Alison. They told me they had already told you of your father's 'friends'! He paused, waiting for a reaction from Form.

"They think they may have handled it rather badly!" He paused again.

"Would you like to talk to me about it?"

Form turned and looked straight into Samuel's eyes. They looked like deep wells. Form could feel the sincerity in them.

Samuel smiled at him. Form bent his head and took a deep breath and sighed.

"Look Samuel, I understand you are considered to be a brilliant man, obviously you are. I also understand about theories and the need for them in order to progress. But if you've got some lame-arsed theory which includes aliens visiting us here and chatting to my Dad and Granddad, then kindly keep it to yourself. I don't wish to be rude but I think it's a pile of shit, in layman's terms, and I don't want to hear anymore. Thank you for a nice evening. I think I'll go and get some rest now. Colin will sort you out, you probably know this place better than I do. I hope you enjoy your stay and the use of the south wing helps your work."

"Will you take the journals?"

"Leave them here in the study. I might look at them some other time." Form strode off haughtily.

Later that night Form could hear Colin and Samuel talking as they came upstairs. He didn't hear all that was said but Colin was definitely flustered and Samuel was calming him down.

Form pondered some kind of conspiracy and lay awake trying to work out just what the purpose of this conspiracy could be. Why did they bother to find him? If they were trying to do him out of his inheritance they could have just not looked for him. Not many knew of his existence. Form didn't know anything about his father. Form started to consider that they might mean what they said!

Out came the brandy again, no, he was not going to go down that road, aliens indeed, he paced around the room. He thought of his dreams in the observatory. He ran to the toilet and vomited.

He phoned Kate, no answer. He phoned David, answer machine. He called down for some chocolate and some warm milk. He paced the room again until Alison came up with his order.

Form didn't recognise himself. He stormed at Alison as soon as she walked in.

"I don't know what your bloody game is, keep your bloody alien shit to yourselves. Tell Professor bloody Herring he can just keep it all to his bloody self and leave me out of it. I don't want any more talk of it from any of you, is that clear? Anyone talking about that shit will be sacked immediately, got it?"

Alison nodded, tears welling up in her eyes. She was visibly shaking.

Form felt some slight remorse for frightening her. He turned away, and finished off almost in a whisper, "Right, go and tell everyone what I've just said, and we'll hear no more of it, OK."

Alison scuttled out of the room, and Form could hear her start to weep as she ran down the corridor. He felt bad, really bad. He returned to the brandy, putting a good dollop in his milk, and curled up in bed eating chocolate. He switched on the telly and watched some programme about idiots on holiday; he kept adding brandy to his milk until he fell asleep.

Form woke up just after three in the morning, feeling pretty bad. He got up and called downstairs. It took a while for anyone to answer the phone.

"Tell Romme I want him to drive me to Kate's. I'll be ready in fifteen minutes. He can meet me at the front entrance."

"Yes, Mr Form, anything else?"

"No, that's it, thank you."

Romme was waiting when Form got to the front entrance. Form got into the back seat and they set off.

As he sat in the car, Form contemplated how easy it had been to get all these people running around after him, but asking no questions. He felt a bit like Al Capone or some big wig gangster. He leant forward and told Romme that he thought he should contact Kate to let her know he was coming. Romme pointed him in the direction of the mobile phone in the back of the car.

Kate took some time to answer the phone. As usual when in a drowsy state she was rather abrupt.

"WHAT?"

"Kate, it's me, I'm on my way over to yours, er, mine, I mean I'm coming over to see you."

"Form, it's flippin'… what time is it?"

"Quarter to four. I need to see you, sorry it's so late."

"Look, Form, I've got work in the morning. Come on over, let yourself in. I'm only working till two, meet me from work. Listen, don't wake me up when you get here, I'm too bloody tired for this. It's not life or death is it?"

"Noooo, it is important, but it can wait, I suppose. Go back to sleep, I'll see you in the morning."

Form felt like a thief creeping into the house at four thirty in the morning. He crept into his old bedroom which suddenly felt safer than it ever had done before. He didn't hear Kate get up in the morning. He only woke with the loud bang as she slammed the front door.

Form was waiting outside the women's refuge at one o'clock. Kate had to run out and bring him in. Men hanging around outside the refuge didn't look good, she explained to him.

Form asked if Kate would mind taking a walk in the park, a picnic somewhere they could talk in private. Kate took a look outside; it wasn't raining but it wasn't exactly picnic weather either. She suggested going to the coffee shop instead. Form was not too keen. "I really wanted some privacy. Let's go home and get a takeaway then, shall we?"

Form ran through the last few days with Kate.

"What do you think, Kate, they're all talking bloody aliens, even the professor, I mean, what is it all about? Why are they doing this?"

Kate had laughed at first but when she had seen that Form was serious she became intrigued. Now she stood up and wandered about the room deep in thought.

"Did they say why?"

"What do you mean, why?"

"Well, why the aliens had contacted them."

"*Kate*!"

"I think you need to read those journals. I think you need to keep an open mind. A lot of stuff that has been invented in that house would have been thought of as just as bizarre as this, in its time!"

"I'm surrounded by bloody loonies, You're not taking this seriously, are you? *Kate... aliens... aliens... we are taking aliens!*"

"*Don't shout at me*! God I wish you were more like your mother... at least she would have given them a chance to explain."

After more to-ing and fro-ing Kate called Colin and got him to send over the journals, and they decided to stay where they were for the weekend. Kate grandly told Colin to tell everyone to have the weekend off. Colin reminded her about the south wing visitors, but thanked her for the thought anyway.

Romme arrived with the journals and a basket of goodies from Tinny. Form said he was sorry to have got Romme up at that ungodly hour. Romme said it was all part of the job and had made things a bit more exciting; anyhow, he had enjoyed the drive back at dawn, very nice and peaceful.

chapter fifteen

Form took his father's journal, and Kate started with his grandfather's. They sat down ready for a long read.

It was not long before Kate asked Form to listen to what she had been reading. "Form, it says here that your grandfather built the chimney to do experiments to see if more energy could be got from fuel with a different approach to the amount of oxygen above. Sounds kooky but plausible. They found that some of the smoke came back down the chimney but was directed to one area. They did experiments with different fuels, coating some wood with what he calls 'the formula'. I think it might be here somewhere. When they lit the fire with the coated wood, the smoke went up and a few minutes later a rock or meteorite came down the chimney."

"And?"

"Well, I suppose that's why Colin didn't want to light that fire! Then he goes on about how they did tests on the rock." She flicked through the pages. "There's tons of calculations and stuff, hold on, they heated the rock to 200 degrees and it exploded," she finished limply.

"So what does that prove? A rock fell out of the chimney, could have been dropped by a bird or something! Most of the stuff in here is about Joshua looking for a material, loads of guff about elasticity and transference. It's all way over my head, some of it looks like hieroglyphics to me!"

"Yeah, a lot of that in here too."

They read on in silence for about half an hour.

"Form, I think this is an important part, you ready?"

"Kate you're talking like you already believe all this!"

"Form, I do in a way, least I want to, look Samuel Herring is…"

Form cut her short.

"I'm surrounded with kooks, Kate you're a lawyer, logical mind and all that, just because some mad professor says so you believe him?"

"I just think we should have an open mind about this and get the facts as they have them before we decide they're all mad. Look, if you were in court with these people, defending them, you'd make sure you had all the facts before you allowed them to be sectioned. None of your family were ever sectioned. Doesn't that say something?"

"Yes, it says that they had so much money they could afford to be mad! You have a point though. What does it say then?"

"Right... so, they tried the coated wood again, and got another rock, blah blah, they did more experiments. Oh! This one exploded as well. I'll look further."

Form left his father's journal. It didn't seem to have anything in it except scientific stuff that he couldn't understand. He hadn't found any personal stuff, or any reference to aliens. He just seemed to waffle on and on about materials with certain properties.

Form went through the basket and laid out some food for them both and made a cup of coffee.

"Aha! This is it, this time, they did it again. This time they put the rock on ice. It says here that the rock formed itself into a platter with markings on it. They tried to decipher the markings. Then they tried it again and this time the platter had different markings. Looks like they did it quite a few times... hold on, here, they did it again and the markings came back in Hindi. What do you think of that?"

"Let me have a look at that."

In the journal were sketches of the platters and the markings on the first few. The last one was sketched with a translation underneath.

"Contact, contact. Send the pulse to confirm contact."

Form looked at the journal turning it upside down. Flicking through the pages, he drummed his fingers on it, and he mulled and mulled. Kate sat on the sofa with her hands drawn in front of her face as if in prayer, tapping her fingers together.

"Do me a favour Kate, can you carry on reading through this while I go for a walk?"

"Sure! Where are you going?"

"Nowhere."

Form was gone for over an hour, Kate was almost busting by the time he returned. She had read a lot further, skipping most of the technical stuff, weaseling out the pertinent bits. It was like an episode of Star Trek she admitted, but to her it all looked pretty real. She was shaking with excitement. She considered being scared, but then decided if this was all real then they couldn't all be baddies, since they had been in contact with Form's family for forty-odd years. All right, there were the two suicides. Kate considered them for a while, and came to the conclusion that Form's father and grandfather were like those fellas in the stock exchange who jumped out of windows when they ballsed up. The type of people who can't take failure. Anyway, they were eccentric; any man who had shacked up with Form's mother had to be eccentric.

As Form entered the house he held up his hand to Kate.

"Don't blast me! Let me settle down first. I've been thinking a lot." He took a deep breath as he sat down, Kate handed him a soft drink, which he accepted with a smile.

"When I was younger my Mum was always on about how when we got visited by higher beings, the rapists of nature would be made to pay and stuff like that. They were always having ceremonies calling to the god of this and the goddess of that. I had tons of it as a kid. You know what it was like when I

139

left them. I mean the way they lived, it was wrong, they did stuff, stuff they shouldn't. All that free love, all the hypocrisy, you know, hating society yet taking their dole cheques and having no intention of ever doing a day's work for it. It's hard. I had an open mind, I closed it, now I have to open it again. All the things I have thought, the way I have lived for years has been doing the right thing! Not living in airy-fairy land like they all did. I've been frightened, frightened of the damage these people can do. They don't mean to, they just go blindly in, not thinking of the consequences. Is that what we're doing now? What if we, well, you know, all this, what if it opens up some kind of gate! Then we find out that they carry some disease that will kill us all! They might not know, they might not mean any harm!"

He looked at her with pleading in his eyes. He wanted an answer, but Kate didn't have one. She shrugged.

"Do you want to hear what I've read?"

"Kate I've got something to tell you! I should have told you years ago, I was afraid you'd hate me. I have to get it off my chest. I think I may have given you AIDS. I'm so sorry." He began to weep.

She came to him and hugged him.

"What on earth gave you that idea, Form? I haven't got AIDS, nor have you. What is this all about?"

"How do you know? I had sex with loads of people. We never used condoms, it was rampant on the commune. I must have picked something up! We were always doing it."

"Form, I had a test two years ago. One of my boyfriends came back from a holiday; he'd had sex with some girl. She wrote to him saying she had HIV so we both got tested. We were clear. I packed him in after that. You must remember, I was sobbing for weeks."

"You never said anything about AIDS."

"Yeah, well, I was embarrassed, you know, been taken for a ride and having to get tested as well, felt a right plonker. So chin up, that's one less worry. This has been bugging you since we broke up, hasn't it? Why didn't you say something? No forget it, I know why you didn't say anything… what are we going to do about this stuff now?"

"Shit, forget that for a bit. So everything's been OK all along. I didn't hurt you?"

"Not physically. You broke my heart, well, sort of cracked it a bit. Staying friends made it easier sometimes, sometimes it made it worse. You did become a bit of an arsehole as well. That made you less attractive, especially when the nose hair thing came along." She smiled. "Glad to see the back of that!"

Form put his hand to his nose.

"Do you want to hear something funny? I thought the nose hair was a symptom of AIDS. I feel a right idiot now."

Kate laughed a big hearty laugh. Form joined in then the two of them huddled together and the hearty laughter turned to tears. They hugged each other and wept and wept. Heart wrenching sobs came from both of them. They stroked each other's hair and wiped tears from their faces. Soon they were wrapped in a passionate kiss, grunting and gasping, their hands on the other's cheeks, pulling themselves closer. Kate pushed Form backwards until he was lying prone on the sofa. Still their lips never parted. They were hungry for one another. Kate started to undress Form. Tugging at his shirt buttons, she moved her lips from his and down his chest. Form tried to wrestle with his trouser belt and pushed them both off the sofa and on to the floor.

"Kate, are you sure this is what you want?"

She knelt up looking straight into his eyes and took his hands in hers.

"Form, you fool, I've always loved you, never stopped. I didn't want to be your best mate, I wanted to be your lover, after all that is a department you're very well trained in! Actually what I really want is to be your wife!" She paused searching his face. "Form... will you marry me, please?"

Form gagged as if he were going to be sick. Kate looked concerned and frightened. Form could see that his reaction was not what she had expected. He coughed and regained himself. He again put her hand in his.

"Kate, if you want me, I can't think why you would, but if you want me, I'll be yours forever. Yes, I'll marry you. I just wish I'd asked years ago."

"Hush, hush, let's not go down regret road, let's just put things right, hubby-to-be!"

She gently took his hand and led him to the bedroom. They undressed each other, slowly, kissing every part of their bodies as they went. Kate did a quick run out to get her handbag for some condoms, giggling as she ran naked across the living room. She dived back into the bed.

"Come on, lover, show me what you're made of!"

chapter sixteen

They lay curled up together in the bed, feeding each other goodies from Tinny's basket, and drinking lemonade (it was the closest they had to champagne). Kate smeared Form's face with dip and then licked it off. Once again they began to kiss passionately. Tightly embracing, they rolled around the bed squashing food all over themselves and the bed. Kate let out thrilled squeals as they rolled around in the dip, chicken salad, grapes, breadsticks and an assortment of vol-au-vents. They made love like hungry animals, pawing, licking, biting each other, loudly grunting, moaning, laughing, squealing and panting late into the night. Ending up bathing together and crawling into Kate's bed exhausted, sleeping wrapped snugly together, both smiling in their dreams. The soft sound of contented breathing in harmony, the only sound in the stillness surrounded by the chaos left from their passion.

"So, Mrs Johnson-to-be! What do we do about these aliens?"

Form was lying on the bed, Kate was sitting cross-legged at the other end of the bed; both were munching toast. They both looked flushed and content, smiles beaming across their faces.

"Let's go back to Stygbees and see Samuel. I think we need to know what he thinks. He'll be able to tell us what is actually happening, won't he?"

"Hope so, I really hope so."

They began to get themselves together, and called for Romme and the car, all the time touching each other at every opportunity, little kisses here and there.

On the journey back they spoke to Romme. He told them he didn't know much about 'the aliens' or 'clever friends' as Joshua used to refer to them. He knew of the search, only Colin, Alison, Tinny and himself knew of the staff members.

Joshua had gone to Hawaii to get his head around it, he had got mugged and Tinny had found him in a bad way. She took him in and cleaned him up. When he felt better he had off-loaded some of the story to them; he seemed to need to tell someone. They had been sceptical but when he had asked them to come to England with him, they had nothing keeping them there, it looked like a good move, so they came over. When they got here, they saw for themselves the truth of the matter and they had stayed with him ever since to try and help.

Joshua had told them that the house had been built on a landing site. The scouts had been left on the planet and they were trying to find the scouts.

"I think the scouts either have had children or they live a much, errr, I don't understand this! They must be hundreds of years old now! I have had it explained to me many times, but nobody knows it all anyway, not even the professor. It is still confusing. The biggest problem is contact. We have problems getting them to explain things. They send messages but we aren't very good at getting messages to them! I'm not a very clever man, Mr Form, I only understand a little bit of it. They need to bring back scouts, I don't know why! We are trying to help them. That's all I know."

On returning to the house they discovered that Samuel was not there but Roger Bagley was. They all got together for a chat. With the help of the journals, Roger explained as much as he could. He told them that Joshua had brought himself and Samuel in as a joint effort. Roger had a hands-on approach, and he was often able to see things that the scientists (he didn't consider himself in that category though most people would) missed. He was able to simplify things. Samuel was a genius, Roger said, as he was the man who interpreted much of the information they received.

Roger took them up to the observatory and then out onto the roof to show them what it was that they were really working on. Once there Form saw that the shelter he had seen from the hot air balloon was a workshop. Inside most of the space was taken up by a sphere, which you could have easily fitted a big space wagon type van in it. It looked sort of like a huge pearl, opaque in colour but it appeared to wobble, tremor would be a better word, as if made of a jelly substance yet as you touched it, it felt solid. Roger made his way to a keyboard. He played one high note and the sphere opened, an opening just appeared in the smooth exterior. Roger motioned them forward to take a look inside. They approached holding each other's hands tightly, excited yet wary. The interior seemed to be moulded, everything looked as though it were joined. Form noticed that from inside the sphere you could see out, all around. Two large seats were in place, moulded and positioned back to back.

"We can get it to spin, but we can't get it to fly yet! We will though, we're really close, really close now," Roger said with pride and excitement in his voice.

Form and Kate didn't say much at all. They climbed inside, dubiously. Roger nodded them on. They sat in the seats and stroked what they assumed were the controls. They just appeared to be dents in the surrounding.

"It won't take off with us in it?" asked Kate.

"No, it's not primed yet, see this well here, this is where we put the primer. That's the problem, we can't get that right yet!"

"And this is going to fly? Where? To outer space? Who's going? What powers it? What is it made of?" Form rattled off a series of questions.

"We think we're going to send someone home! Sounds mad doesn't it! We don't know who yet, when we find out who, we might have some more answers, we think. But we also think that the who doesn't know that they are the who! If you get my drift. Big problem there. As far as Samuel can make out they think they are humans, they definitely live in England - something to do with a need to be on the same land mass. This place sends out some wave patterns, talk to Samuel on that one, not my area. The only thing we know for sure is that they are sensitive to vibrations, sounds and get physically "home sick" when away. Sound like anyone you know?" he ended with a laugh.

Form and Kate were stunned and amazed by the sphere. They spoke to each other of the wonderment of it all. Form thought a lot about his mother. She would have loved this, something completely wild, just up her street. The whole situation seemed incredible to them both. They spent the next few hours talking to Roger and Colin about how this had all come about, pondering on the now answered question of life on other planets. Why couldn't they just come down and pick up their scouts? What did they look like? What do they really want? Perhaps biggest of all, how had this been kept secret for so long? If these beings have been here so long, how could they not know they were not human? So many questions without answers. Colin had a theory based on an episode of Star Trek he had seen.

"I think the beings are using humans as hosts, that they have transferred themselves to other hosts as the human bodies have become old or died, like a Dax, I think that was the name of it, on Star Trek." Colin smiled a smug smile that indicated that he thought himself rather smart with this theory.

"So you think they live forever?" said Kate.

"Well, they've been looking for them for a long time. They were obviously here before the house was built. I mean, the house was built over four hundred years ago!"

They all stood nodding at Colin, all umming and erring in agreement. The conversation carried on well into the night, well lubricated with alcohol, which led them into an intense discussion and then a procession of impersonations of what the beings might be like, then into who they might be: the man who runs the local newsagents near Form's; Jimmy Saville; the Queen Mum (who seemed to live forever); Jeremy Beadle amongst other prospective candidates.

The work in the laboratory became very exciting to Form and Kate. They both wanted to spend every spare moment with Roger and the students (the students were unaware of exactly what they were working on - they believed they were looking for a new power source - which was kind of the truth!). Alison brought it to their attention that Jamie might become curious of this sudden interest and recommended that they make an effort to expand their interests.

With that in mind and after some discussion they decided to announce their intention to get married. The whole house was ecstatic for them both, and the champagne once again made an appearance! The band Supergrass who were recording in the studio offered to make a record for them to be played at the wedding. Kate was thrilled at the prospect, Form less so. They had both sat in on some of the recording sessions, and the band had proven to be very friendly (hardly surprising, thought Form, as they were being given everything they could possibly want). The band had been invited to share dinner with them three times in this last week. Although Form found them to be very amusing, he did not enjoy their music overly much. He had told them so, and one evening he had gone as far as suggesting changes to them. Kate had found this hilarious as Form could not be described as a musical genius in any way. She put his new found knowledge down to the six tequila slammers he had been manoeuvred into having!

With this up and coming event Jamie was swamped with tasks. He rushed around the house with portfolios of dress designers, and wedding organizers. He went backwards and forwards to London trying to find the perfect everything. Form and Kate kept him busy by not giving him any idea of what they wanted and pooh poohing every one of his suggestions. They sent him off to France, Ireland, The Bahamas and other places in search of the perfect wedding.

David had been over the moon with the news too, offering help in the music department. One weekend when he came to stay he also suggested a double wedding, which earned him a slapped face as he had not mentioned a thing to Sarah!

"Who the hell does he think he is, imagine, he thought I'd just swoon and say, 'Why David how wonderful of you to love me so,' huh! He only says he loves me when he's drunk. Even then he tells everyone he loves them when he's drunk. The doorman at Stringfellows was his greatest friend ever last month!" With this she stormed off shortly followed by Kate to try and calm things down.

Jamie dutifully made the proper announcements in the proper newspapers and magazines. They refused offers from OK and Hello magazines to cover the event, much to Jamie's disgust. To keep Jamie happy they agreed to an engagement party. This time it was to be a formal event and all the 'Names' that Jamie was dying to invite were allowed. He was chuffed. All old friends were invited and assisted with correct dress etc. for an occasion such as this. Form and Kate were surprised at how little they had to do in all these arrangements. Jamie immersed himself, just occasionally checking with them to get their approval.

While Jamie was amused elsewhere Form and Kate were free to poke their noses into the goings on in the laboratory. Samuel had returned briefly. He was a man much in demand. He found it very frustrating but felt that if he gave too much time to the project it would create interest from areas they could do without. They all agreed with this, but it did mean things often had to be on hold for some time.

148

Samuel was very pleased to hear of Form's acceptance of the situation and kept in touch with Form on a regular basis via e-mail. Roger had moved in permanently to the house and worked like a man possessed at times; other times he sat for long periods thinking and getting very grumpy if disturbed. He had exhibited to Form and Kate how they got the sphere to spin and almost hover! The primer was put into the well in the sphere and connected to a machine that measured stress levels in metals. It caused vibrations to be passed through it at different levels. At one level the sphere began to spin slowly round and round. Roger had found that connecting the vibration machine through the electronic organ made the sphere hover about half an inch above the floor. It was very exciting. All the vibrations gave an all over body massage, at first slightly unnerving, then leading to a feeling of complete relaxation. Form and Kate enjoyed this. Roger on the other hand found this quite irritating as he found it impossible to work for hours after any test run.

chapter seventeen

Jamie had enjoyed every minute of making these elaborate preparations. He had organised beautiful gold embossed invitations, two adjoining rooms had huge tables running the length of them both, crystal and gold, fine china and ornamental displays running throughout, floral displays and new lighting with a definite Victorian feel to it all. Three classical quintets were to be scattered about and a stage had been erected in the garden leading off one of the main eating areas for Supergrass to put on a show. The garden was also a decorative extravaganza of flowers, torches and lighting. Masses of new staff had been called in, new uniforms for all, maintaining the Victorian theme. Throughout the week the house was inundated with cards, bouquets, messages of good wishes, mainly from people neither Form nor Kate knew. They had insisted that on the invitations a request should be made for no presents. Instead the women's refuge had again been nominated to benefit from anyone's desire to show their good wishes. Kate had been informed by the refuge that they had received over ten thousand pounds. It was noted that most of the donations had come from agencies that they both agreed were trying to butter Form up for some reason or another.

Kate called David and told him of their plans for the party. He was encouraged to alter his dress plans along with Sarah. They giggled on the phone. Every time Kate saw Jamie running around in the throes of his preparations she would snigger. Form noted her doing this and queried her motives for their outfits.

"Are you just having a go at Jamie? What's he done?"

"Well... you know, he's a bit pompous, you know, a suck up to all those la de da's. I think it will bring him down a peg or two."

"Don't you think it's a bit cruel?"

"Yes, but he should loosen up. He's working for you after all. He keeps trying to tell us how to act, who's important? I mean, who's important! He doesn't know who's important to us, know what I mean? Come on, Form," she whined, "don't be a pooper, it'll be a laugh, yes, Jamie will be raging but hey! It's our party not his!"

Form reluctantly agreed. He did dislike the way Jamie tried to push him into 'Society'. It held no appeal to him. Yes, it was their party and he would have just the kind of fun he liked!

chapter eighteen

(The day of the Engagement party)

Form and Kate were woken by a very excited and flustered Colin.

"You have to come, you have to come now, it's amazing, it's all happening, now, it's all happening now!" Colin's voice worked its way into a high squeak.

Both Form and Kate were now bolt upright in bed, shaking sleep from their heads.

"What's happened? Has it flown off? Is Roger there?" fumbled Kate.

"It's all starting now, you must come and see. Roger sent me to get you. Shall I meet you there?" he quickly replied, obviously urgently wanting to return to the lab.

"No, wait, wait for us, we're coming, right now, we're coming," said Form as he and Kate scrambled out of bed and threw on dressing gowns, hurriedly following Colin out of the door.

As they entered the lab, Roger was approaching the door.

"Ah you're here, good, we have to move it."

"What has happened?" Form asked.

"Didn't Colin explain?"

"Explain! Explain what? How was I supposed to explain?" stuttered Colin.

Roger looked at the bewildered Form and Kate. "I do apologise. Once I've got the bit between my teeth, I sometimes forget to keep everyone up to date, so, yes, let's sit down, it'll be good for me to run through it."

Roger turned to Tom, his assistant, a very cool calm laid back student who had been Roger's shadow for months; he seemed to be harnessing the sphere.

"Come on, Tom, sit down, let's take a moment to catch our breath, shall we?"

"Whatever you say, prof, I'm not 100% sure that I'm awake anyway."

"Alison has gone to fetch Romme and Tinny. Could we wait for them please?" asked Colin.

Form and Kate scanned the lab. Apart from being partly harnessed, the sphere looked no different, there were no aliens about (well, no obvious ones). Kate tapped Form on the shoulder and pointed to the far wall which seemed to be littered with paper. They both shrugged.

"Yes, yes, of course," replied Roger he sat down at the table and gave a big sigh.

Form turned to Tom. "Are you all right?"

"Now that is a question I'm not sure I'm qualified to answer right now."

"Why, what happened?" Form persisted.

"Can you wait till the others get here, Form?" asked Kate.

"Yes, sorry, I just, yes, I'll wait," they tailed off into a big empty silence.

They all jumped visibly as Colin's mobile phone pierced the silence.

He looked at his phone nonplussed. Who would be calling him at this hour? He got up and walked away from the table as he answered the call.

"Hello, oh, Hello Ned... yes, unexpected yes... I see, how strange, an urge... Well, yes, it could well be... as soon as you like Ned... Right, see you soon then." he hung up and turned to them, his face alight with excitement.

He started to gush. "That was Ned, my nephew. I think they are involved with the 'friends.' He says he felt a calling to come here, an irresistible urge. I've told him to come over, he's part of it. I sort of thought they were involved, wasn't 100% before though."

Roger did not look best pleased "Don't you think we should keep the number of people who know about this to a minimum?"

Form, Kate and Tom showed surprise at Colin's statement.

"That is not always in our hands, Roger. The call has gone out. You have to let in those who answer the call!"

Alison's flushed face appeared around the door. She had obviously been moving faster than her usual stately amble. She was followed in by Tinny and Romme both looking just as flushed.

Quick greetings were exchanged and they all sat down to listen to Roger.

"Well, as you know, we've been experimenting with sound waves, tried an assortment of pitches etc, then tonight, I wanted to monitor responses from outside, so Tom sat in, wearing his headphones, listening to the radio, and whoosh, it all happened." Roger threw his arms wide, and his eyes looked ready to pop from their sockets.

"A huge pulse of light blasted from all directions, wind knocked me off me feet, the sphere hovered about four feet off ground." Roger gushed at them, excited to tell the tale at last.

They all looked at Tom; he returned their looks with a dazed grin and a nod.

"So how did it stop?" asked Kate.

"I jumped and pulled my headphones off and knocked my walkman on the floor and it turned off, then the sphere just slowly stopped," replied Tom in a quite matter-of-fact tone.

"Yes, surprisingly gentle landing after such an explosive take off," mumbled Roger to himself.

"So it just did it once?" asked Form.

"Yes, I think we need to take it to the chimney to try it again," said Roger. "That's why I called for Colin. We need to move the sphere now before morning, while no one's about."

"Come on, Tom, Romme and I will show you how. We've done this once or twice before."

Everyone stood up, Form, Kate and Alison making offers of help.

"It's easier with three," said Colin.

Positioning Romme at the front of the sphere and Tom at the rear, Colin took hold of the harness-like reins from behind. Romme lifted the sphere with little effort and Colin guided Tom to hold down his end as it rose. Once they established a steady balance Colin took the reins to guide from side to side. Romme and Tom lightly pushed the sphere and it glided towards the freight lift.

Kate gave an excited 'whoop' as the sphere moved and clutched Form's arm. He grinned at her and patted her hand.

"The main problem is stopping it from just spinning once it's moving," Colin explained.

The others all ran up to the observatory as soon as Colin shut the gates of the massive freight elevator.

As Form and Kate arrived Colin was manoeuvring the sphere towards the chimney.

"It's not going to fit," said Form limply.

"Oh no!" cried Kate.

"Put it down, Colin, we're going to have to work this one out," said Roger.

Romme moved away from the sphere as did Tom, and Colin put the reins down while trying to ensure the sphere was steady. The sphere seemed to be still being pushed. Colin scanned around it, the sphere moved forward toward the chimney, slowly at first then as if it had been sucked enthusiastically in through a straw, it was inside the chimney! The air in the room seemed to be pulled into the chimney too and everyone lurched as the gust of air passed them by.

"Blimey," said Colin, "it's never done that before!"

"You don't say," said Roger sarcastically.

"Whoa, what happened there!" exclaimed Tom.

"Did you feel the electricity when that happened?" asked Kate.

Tinny and Alison were hugging each other in both excitement and fear.

The air in the room seemed to remain static and everyone's hair stood on end, making them all look like crazed clowns.

"Does anyone know what we are supposed to be doing here?" asked Form in a rather shaky voice.

"I know some," ventured Colin. "I have been a host. I think I need to tell you all about it." He looked around at them all.

"A host? What do you mean?" asked Tom.

Colin looked unsettled. "Listen, can we go to the lab and away from here, all this static, it's…. we can't do anymore for the time being anyway."

"But I want to check it out in the chimney," said Rodger.

"Later, Roger, can we please all go to the lab," returned Colin giving Roger a tired look.

He made his way out, Alison and Tinny following closely behind him, seeming eager to get away.

"It's all very well talking about this, all this time, but I thought I'd be braver by now," Colin muttered to Alison. "All of a sudden I'm exhausted."

She stroked his shoulder. "You're doing wonderfully. We are all afraid, you're not the only one, and you're not in charge so if the shit hits the fan, darling, it will totally bypass you." She smiled and hugged him.

He took comfort in her embrace.

Roger, obviously torn between wanting to stay with the sphere and needing to know all that Colin had to tell, huffed and puffed his way to the door, beckoning the others as he went.

By the time they all got to the lab, they were all showing signs of being physically drained, flopping onto chairs, sighing and closing their eyes.

Alison stirred herself. "Is there any rush at the moment?" she asked Colin.

"What for?" he replied.

"Well, I was just thinking that I really need a cup of tea." She grinned at him and scrunched her shoulders.

"Good idea!" piped up Tom enthusiastically.

Everyone settled themselves down and Tinny joined Alison in making tea, filling the kettle and searching for cups. Roger paced.

Colin's phone rang again.

"Hello!" he said enthusiastically.

"The boys are just coming up to the gate, Romme, can you go and let them in please. Two more cups, Alison. Ned and Leo are here."

Kate nearly fell off her chair when she saw Leo walk through the door.

Leo and Ned, she instantly recognised them. By Tom's face he did too.

Form obviously had no idea. Ned and Leo Granger, the bad boy brothers of the super group 'Pondlife'! Kate could not believe her eyes.

"These are his nephews? He never said," whispered Kate to Form.

Form gave her a puzzled look. Why would he? He thought.

Leo swaggered into the room, and held his arms wide as if greeting an audience.

"We've come to make music, the Muse has hit us, miracles are going to happen tonight!" he grandly announced.

"Shut up, you Muppet," mumbled Ned.

"Oh, I do hope so," Kate replied to Leo's announcement.

"Leo, Ned," Alison warmly greeted them.

"For f**ks sake," said Tom.

"What's this all about?" asked Roger.

"These are my nephews, Mr Form." Colin turned and indicated Ned and Leo and nodded toward Roger. "Roger," he said.

Ned moved forward to Form offering his hand to shake as Leo was wrapped in a hug from Alison.

"Sorry to just land ourselves on ya. Heard you're the new Lord of Manor. I want you to know, me uncle doesn't usually just let us turn up in middle of night. I mean, this isn't normal, he hasn't been takin' the piss or anything?"

Form was flummoxed. "Err, I'm sure, well, nice to have you here." They shook hands awkwardly.

Tom hovered behind Form obviously wanting to be introduced to the brothers. He jutted his hand forward and shook Ned's hand. "I'm Tom, you're great, thanks," he muttered.

Ned laughed. "Chill out, mate, we're only blokes."

"I'm sorry, am I being rude, are you famous?" asked Form.

"What planet have you been on?" exclaimed Leo loudly.

"We're almost as big as God, or should I call him Mr Lennon?" He laughed at his own joke. Kate tittered, and Leo flashed her a smug glance.

"Pondlife!" exclaimed Tom. "They are Pondlife."

Form's blank expression told the story.

Kate gave a sigh. "You really have been on another planet, haven't you, Form?"

Roger coughed. "Another planet is where we may all be going or receiving visitors from!" he said pointedly, trying to bring the subject away from the brothers whom he saw as an irritating distraction.

"Wow, what is this place?" asked Ned as he strolled into the lab proper and took in the enormous equipment. "Is this England's NASA?"

Tom skipped forward and put his arm around Ned's shoulder. He made a sweeping gesture around the lab. "Welcome to my world. The shit that's going on here, you won't believe, you are so gonna write a song about tonight, I'm telling ya."

Ned felt Tom's excitement, looked him up and down, and smiled. "Bring it on, bring it on."

Roger took command again, eager to get moving.

"Can everyone gather at the table, please. Alison has everyone's cup of tea," he rolled his eyes, "perhaps we could get on with the business in hand. Colin, we need to know the story, now!" he sighed, and took a breath "please."

Kate grabbed Form and whispered to him as they reassembled around the table. "Pondlife, biggest band since The Beatles, been going for 'bout ten years. |The brothers are always fighting, all over the papers every day, all the time. Where have you been?" she looked at him in bewilderment.

"I'm sorry, I obviously should have read Hello magazine more often!" he replied sarcastically.

"You should have just opened your eyes," she countered with a sneer and sat down with a smug grin.

"I think it's best if I explain it all to the boys," he indicated Ned and Leo, "tell them all I know, as it'll clear things up for all of us." He paused. "OK?"

"Just get on with it," mumbled Roger.

"Shut up!" Form snapped at Roger.

Roger gave Form an angry glance and stood up, then sat down again.

Muttering, encouraging Colin to tell his tale, came from the others.

Tinny pushed a cup of tea in front of Roger. He sneered at her, and she shrugged her shoulders and poked her tongue out at him.

"Well Ned, Leo, this is a bit unbelievable," started Colin.

"You're not being punk'd or anything," butted in Tom.

"Thanks for that, Tom," laughed Ned. "But it would have to be some kinda punk to make me and Leo both wake up in the middle of night and know exactly that we both had to come here. So that's pretty weird, what else weird you got, Unc?"

"Plenty," said Kate.

"Yeah, plenty," agreed Colin and Tom together.

Leo spread his arms wide and leant back in his seat. "Lay it on me, Unc."

"Right, here we go. Aliens, we're dealing with aliens," he looked to see Leo and Ned's response.

"We're still listening, Unc," said Ned.

Leo nodded.

"The aliens have been here for a long time, couple of hundred years. The family have been helping them for a long time. There are a few of them, they move from host to host, but the host doesn't die or anything," he looked around. "It's not like Night of the Body Snatchers."

"What is it like?" asked Form. "You said you were a host."

"I didn't know I was a host until it left me. I knew something was different, but it just seemed like," he shrugged, "like the penny had dropped, strange really. It's like having a revelation, all of a sudden. All of a sudden I was sure of myself, I seemed to know what to do, whatever I put my hand to, things just made sense easier." His face became slightly flushed and he gained a twinkle in his eye. "Yes, I just became," he shrugged, "the best I can be!" He looked around? "Does that make sense?"

"No," said Roger, but it was muffled by the resounding 'yes's' from Ned and Leo.

"When we walked into the studio to record 'Tell us the Tale Annabelle' we was filled wiv supreme confidence, supreme. People thought we was just cocky kids, I s'pose we were, but we *knew,* we just *knew,* it was superb. We talked about it all the time. One minute we were happy to be guided by the company and just do what they said to get a hit, next thing, we knew *exactly* what to do and we knew we couldn't be wrong, total surety, amazing," gushed Ned, Leo fervently nodding his agreement.

"Yes, that's it, total surety," nodded Colin

"I can't imagine how wonderful that must feel," sighed Kate.

The others nodded, and mumbled agreement.

"It only seems to apply to the stuff you're good at though. It certainly never increased our kid's or my ability to avoid cocking things up off stage or outside the studio."

"Well, as I said, it's not like the invasion of the body snatchers. You're still you, just more certain."

"You said you know it when it goes," said Ned. "Does that mean, we have still got them? Coz I ain't felt it leave!"

"Yes, I think you still do. When mine left, it was like it left a video tape on fast forward in my head. In the blink of an eye, I had the whole picture of what they had been doing, the time it had taken to communicate with us, the search for materials to build the ship, the desire for them to finish this project," replied Colin. "And I think they are calling them all in now. You boys need to see the machine."

"There's a machine? Whoa, great!" exclaimed Leo.

"You are just so gonna love the machine," Tom gushed at Leo.

Halfway up the stairs to the conservatory Leo's whole body suddenly jerked.

"Whoa! What was that?" This was mirrored by Ned almost simultaneously. Everyone exchanged glances; no one seemed to have anything to say. Leo nodded his head onward and they all followed.

The door to the observatory opened heavily; the atmosphere inside seemed somehow thicker. Leo walked into the observatory enwrapped in the feeling the thick atmosphere had on his body, twisting and turning his arms in the air, smiling and giving an agreeable nod. Tom followed him in, taking the stance of someone facing into a strong wind and waded through the air. Ned at first took the same stance as Leo, but as he turned from the door he looked up to see the screen of stars covering the crystal dome.

"Is this a black hole?" he asked almost in a whisper.

Roger passed him, making his way determinedly to the fireplace, frantically tapping at a hand held device. "I doubt very much that you want me to tell you how ridiculous that statement was!" His irritation at being out of control on this project showed clearly.

"I *do* apologise Mr Professor," sneered Ned and returned to gazing mesmerized at the ceiling.

Roger and Tom made their way to their monitors and machines laid on the table. The others hovered in the doorway watching Leo and Ned eating in the atmosphere and 'feeling' the air around them.

The fireplace caught Leo's eye. The sphere, larger than the opening, made it appear like a pearlised tunnel.

"What is that!" he exclaimed.

Tom laughed. "I told you, you were going to love it, this is *it*!" He made his way to the fireplace beckoning Leo and Ned to follow, and the others followed suit.

Kate held onto Form's arm tightly. She leant up to his ear and whispered, "I feel really horny," but the sound seemed to carry through the air and everyone heard. Form and Kate both gave an embarrassed glance at everyone. Form coughed loudly.

Leo made an exaggerated grab to his crotch. "I know what you mean, my balls are ready to bust!" Leo, Ned and Tom all laughed. Alison made a playful swipe at Leo and tapped him on the shoulder.

"You mind your mouth Mister. You're not too big for a smacked bum," she said.

Ned waggled his bottom at Alison and mockingly said, "Oh me first, Auntie Ally." She laughed and tapped him on the bottom.

After a time spent circling the machine, feeling the steady flow of energy that slid from it, peering up the chimney stack, wondering and amazing at all that they saw, Ned suddenly announced that it was time to get the show on the road. They all looked to Roger for guidance.

"Well, I think the first move to make should be for one of you boys to get into the machine with Tom's walkman, playing the same tune, and monitor what happens! We should feel a large force, the machine should rise quite quickly to about four feet high, possibly more. We know that by throwing out the walkman the machine came to a gentle stop before, so I should imagine that is your brake." He looked at Ned and Leo "Not much to give you really, is it!"

"Professor, there is a CD player within the machine; we don't need to use the walkman." Tom, endeavouring to be helpful, reminded Roger.

"Yes, I am well aware of that, thank you Tom!" Roger replied snappily. "But I think initially as a trial run, it's best to re-enact the experiment as it was before."

Tom rolled his eyes at Leo, and Leo giggled like a schoolboy in class.

"What were you listening to?" asked Leo.

"You're gonna hate me," replied Tom.

"Come on, what was it, I bet I know what it was." They exchanged glances.

"Ray Warbler," they chorused.

"Oh, do be real," whined Ned. "Any bloody tosspot but not him!"

Tom gave Ned an apologetic grimace. "I've been practising 'Nymphette's' for a karaoke party I'm going to!"

Kate laughed and explained to Form that there was a long running feud between the boys and this other pop star.

Tinny piped in. "Ray's a lovely boy, now, you two, leave him alone, you hear?"

"You know Ray?" Kate asked Tinny.

"Oh yes, lovely boy, been here a few times," she giggled. "He can't stay here too long, he loves my cooking too much, he gets fat," she giggled.

"Yeah, fat lardy-arsed gay boy wannabe," muttered Ned under his breath, but as before when Kate had whispered, they all heard him. He glanced around guiltily. "He irritates the crap outa me, what can I say?" he said and held his hands up.

chapter nineteen

Leo stepped back as Roger pushed a key on his keyboard on the table and the door of the sphere appeared. He leant in cautiously scanning the interior.

He coughed nervously "Right, walkman," he held his hand out and Tom gave him the walkman.

As he slid into the seat the sphere began to emanate a deep droning noise. Leo looked at Tom quizzically.

"No, that didn't happen before," said Tom

Leo took a big deep breath, and closed his eyes. "It's OK, right, I'll carry on"

"Hey, our kid!" called out Ned. "If this thing explodes, can I have the Smash hits award from your loo?"

"It's superglued to the window sill, but you can have the whole window if you like, tosser!" Leo responded.

Leo turned on the walkman! A *huge* surge of air pulled everyone towards the fireplace, the sphere shot up into the chimney stack, the room was filled with bright pinky-white light, the air thickened visibly, and as suddenly as it rose, the sphere returned to its former resting place and came to a gentle bobbing halt.

They stumbled forward with heavy movements to see Leo emerging from the sphere, flushed, dazed and smiling.

He turned directly to Ned. "Come on, we've both gotta do it, and we should play our own music. It'll be best if we don't use the walkman. Come on, chop chop, let's get moving. Tom, get one of our CDs, will ya!"

"Yup, no problem!" Tom replied and with a skip turned round and as much as the air would allow him, ran out of the observatory.

Kate began giggling as she watched Tom trying to run. Colin joined her. A titter ran through them all. Ned and Leo began to emulate Tom's running, only to find how difficult it was.

Ned and Leo settled into the sphere which deepened its humming to a bass sound that vibrated through everyone, put the CD of their masterpiece album 'Tell the Tale Annabelle' in place, and grasped each other's hand. Leo pressed the button.

This time the surge of air was immense. Tinny and Romme were thrown forward and collided with the fireplace. The table and its contents smashed against the wall, but seemed to bounce. Tinny's screams turned into a puzzled, "Oh!"

Form, Kate, Colin, Alison, Roger and Tom were all curled in a variety of positions on the ground. They all had been swept four or five feet across the floor. They gradually uncurled and looked around. The whole room was bathed in the pinky-white light, but this time, the air was visibly thick, deep heavy waves could be seen snaking through the room, emanating from the fireplace and slowly, smoothly working its way up to the very top of the crystal dome, like fluffy clouds of pink candy floss.

Zombie like, they rose and wandered aimlessly around.

"Where are the boys?" asked Alison suddenly.

Everyone's attention flew back to the fireplace, which appeared empty; thick energy waves smoothly flowed from it, but there was no sign of the sphere. They slowly moved closer, cautiously, fighting the density of the air, exchanging worried glances, then distracted by the air waves and coating themselves in it, shook themselves in reverie, and moved closer still.

Gently the bottom of the sphere came into view at the top of the fire place. They all sighed as it settled back to its light bobbing parking position.

The doors opened and the boys lay prostrate in their seats, relaxed and smiling. Leo turned to Roger, who was first by his

166

side. "Better than the best sex I've *ever* had!" He grinned at Ned. "Did the earth move for you too, bruv?"

"F**kin right it did, Jeesusss, I dunno if I can walk!" he exclaimed laughing.

"Jelly legs."

Everyone moved as if in slow motion as they waded through the thick electric air. Ned and Leo joined the others outside the fireplace. They answered the quizzical looks with broad grins.

"I FEEL GREAT!" exclaimed Ned enthusiastically and threw himself into the air as if jumping on a soft bed. He was supported! They all gasped, including Ned.

"I'm floating man! I'm floating, look, look, I'm floating."

"Wot the f**k! That is unreal." Leo reacted in a high pitched squeak.

Tom gave a lurch and threw himself in a similar fashion to Ned. The air supported him for a second, then he slowly sank through the air until he was gradually lowered to the ground.

"Hey, I'm floating," he exclaimed. "Oh I think I'm sinking, hey, this is so cool." He flapped his arms slightly. "So how come you're floating. What are you doing, Ned?"

"Nothing, I'm doing nothing, I'm just bloody floating." He laughed. "Our kid, you try."

Leo leaned backwards into the air. It supported him, and he leant further.

"This feels so weird."

"Lift your feet up," said Roger watching the proceedings before him with wonder, reaching for a note pad.

Tom groaned loudly with the effort of getting back up from the floor.

"Everyone, just lie into it, it feels fantastic."

Tinny and Alison, giggling side by side, were the first to take Tom's advice. Boldly they held each other's hands and leant back into the air. They squealed almost in terror as they lifted their feet, followed by a surprised gasp as they momentarily floated. They giggled and muttered, "This is nice," as they sank down slowly to the floor. Form and Kate followed suit. Colin, Romme and Roger watched excitedly. Leo lifted his feet.

"Hey, hey, hey, hey, I'm f**kin floating, woo hoo, bro, this is supreme, this is supremo, my f**kin God supreme!"

"Look at that," exclaimed Tom. "How are you doing it?" and he launched himself again into the air, floating momentarily and again sinking to the floor. He growled, "What am I doing wrong?"

"It's coz we're hosts, Tom, *WE* are superhuman!" said Ned haughtily

And then he emphasised his theory by twisting around. He dipped slightly causing him to give an unsteady, "Whoa!" but he remained floating.

Tom adopted a serious tone. "Do you reckon you could fly?"

Leo adopted a 'Superman' pose and tried to launch himself forward, but he just seemed to lean, in slow motion. He tried again; Ned tried too.

"Nah," said Leo disappointedly

"It's more like tryin' to crawl over the softest lightest snuggliest f**kin' mattress that covers f**kin' everything," said Ned.

"Still, that is so cool," said Tom admiringly.

For a while they launched themselves into the air, Colin, Romme and Roger being reluctant at first but like children doing it again, again, again after their initial trepidation. Kate and Form launched themselves together and turned to face one another, kissing as they sank down.

"Kissing on air," Kate seductively whispered to Form.

As Romme leant back, Tinny launched herself on top of him. They squealed and giggled as they lowered to the floor with a playful wrestle.

"Tinny!" squealed Alison as she rose through the air, Colin lightly holding the base of her back. "It's like I weigh nothing!" Colin slid his hand down and gently stroked Alison's bottom. She turned to him with a coy smile, which he returned with a jaunty raise of the eyebrow.

"Right!" said Ned "Enough horseplay, children, we have much to do, and so little time!" he continued dramatically.

"And I'm starving," added Leo.

Roger sighed as he entered the lab and held his hand to his head. "That much electrical activity messes your head up."

"Made me f**kin' horny," stated Leo, with another grope of his crotch.

Colin and Alison entered arm in arm. Colin with a rising sense of urgency, took command.

"It's half past four, the kitchen starts rousing in an hour." He nodded at Tinny and said, "You better be off, keep everything as normal as possible."

Without hesitation Romme and Tinny made off out of the lab.

"We are going to have lots of visitors very soon. We have to keep it as quiet as we can. We are also going to be very busy, so I suggest that right now as many people get as much sleep as they can."

"I'll second that one, Unc, but I need some food, got a major appetite going on here. I feel like I haven't eaten for months!" declared Leo, ending in a whine.

"There's loads of packets of biscuits by the kettle for now Leo. Tinny will sort some food out as soon as she can," Alison reassured him.

Leo launched himself toward the biscuits with gusto.

Form and Kate hurried along the corridor, sexual tension seeping from every pore. Their arms wrapped around each other,

169

wanting to be touching, touching every part. They stopped and entered a passionate embrace, kissing wildly, then they hurried along the corridor. As they turned the corner their eyes met with the vision of Tinny and Romme locked in a passionate embrace against the far wall, Tinny's bottom sitting very neatly in the bottom impression on the wall. Romme pulled up suddenly as he heard their footsteps approaching. An awkward silence, both couples seemed to just shrug and go their separate ways in one movement.

Romme gave Colin a knowing wink as he entered the kitchen. Tinny was serving him up egg on toast and she ruffled his hair as she turned back to the cooker. Colin straightened his tie, coughed and winked back at Romme, skipped around behind Tinny and picked up a piece of toast.

"Ally's just picking up the rotas and delivery schedules from the office. Food going up to the lab?" Colin asked Tinny nodding towards the rows of bacon cooking.

"Yes, two of the girls are already in. I've sent them to the stores to refill the dorm cupboards. I made it very casual when I told them about Ned and Leo. They know the protocol with visitors anyway so they'll be fine, but they were so excited. I do hope they can keep their ditzy heads and actually work today! Not much chance of keeping their presence quiet from that other one, Amy, she's so ditzy, just the type to text her friends and bring the paparazzi charging down and there's already so much to do!"

Colin nodded. "Yes, we need to run like a well oiled machine. I feel more like a worn out rusty old tractor right now though," he laughed.

Romme laughed. "I feel more like taking you back to bed," he said grabbing Tinny around the waist and spinning her.

She giggled coyly. "Get off me, you big baboon."

Colin's phone rang. "Hi, Ned, food's almost on its way," he said lightly.

"Oh did you.... Yes, yes, of course... How long? Yes that's fine." He turned to Tinny. "How long for the food?"

"Ten minutes," she replied.

"Ten minutes, two of the staff will bring it up. They're very excited about meeting you two," he sighed, "it might be a good idea to butter them up a bit and tell them you're avoiding the dreaded pap. They'll be on their best behaviour if they think they are saving your butts!"

As the first light of morning arrived, a large black Range Rover made its way up the gravel driveway, mist swirling around the tyres as the crunching sound cut through the silence. Colin looked out of the window. He smiled, possibly the most famous Range Rover in England currently. 'I bet they think they are incognito, he thought.

Romme made his way down the entrance steps to greet the visitors. As she alighted from the Range Rover, Maybelline gushed at Romme.

"Hello, darling," she drawled "We're here for the party! I swear, my whole life has been leading up to this point. Take us to your leader, my good man!" she ended with a chuckle.

"May!" cried Greg. "

"What?"

"Lower the drama meter, will ya," he replied.

She gave him a withering look.

Romme smiled inside. Maybelline and Greg Rigsby were famous for the tempestuousness of their relationship. Maybelline, the world famous pop diva, and Greg Rigsby, the talented Brit art film director, two very explosive artistic characters, which made for a very entertaining marriage.

Colin put the phone down and turned to Alison and Tinny both sitting at the kitchen table.

"Well, they think of everything. Looks like we are going to get some professional help!"

Alison and Tinny looked at him puzzled. "Well?" said Alison.

"*That*, my dear, was none other than our First lady!"

"First lady what?" she asked

He rolled his eyes "The Prime Minister's wife, you dafty!"

"Ooo!" Alison and Tinny both responded, suitably impressed.

"She's on her way, coming by helicopter, should be here in about forty minutes!"

Tinny stood up "Oh God, so much to do!" and she twirled around in a light panic.

Maybelline squealed with delight when she laid eyes on Ned and Leo in the lab. They turned from the two giggling housemaids in response to her squeal.

"MAY!" shouted Leo and swung his arms wide to catch her as she threw herself into his embrace.

The two housemaids went into rapturous delight at the sight of Maybelline and Greg, jumping up and down and clapping their hands, giving excited little squeaks, holding on tightly to the napkins they had just got Ned and Leo to sign for them. Seeing Romme there (and knowing the house rules about requesting autographs) the girls quickly regained their composure and hurried out, huddled together in excited whispering.

Colin knocked on Form's bedroom door and waited to be invited in.

Form and Kate were lying in reverie after some very passionate lovemaking and jumped at the knock on the door.

"Come in," called Form, scrambling into a respectable posture. Kate giggled and snuggled down into the bed.

"Sorry to disturb you, Mr Form, I was hoping you might be able to get a few hours' sleep, but I thought I should inform you of the latest happenings."

"Yes, yes, of course, Colin, what's happened?" asked Form with concern.

"Well, we have some more visitors." He looked at Kate knowing she would be more impressed than Form by who the new visitors were.

Kate sat up.

"Mr Greg Rigsby and his wife Maybelline have just arrived. They have gone straight to the lab with Romme."

"*Oh, my God,*" screeched Kate.

Colin grinned.

This time even Form couldn't be ignorant of Maybelline, and he was just as surprised as Kate and copied her statement.

"We also have another visitor on their way, Chardonnay Blythe!" Colin couldn't help but put a touch of blasé into his voice.

Form gasped and shook his head

"No way!" said Kate.

"Yes, way," replied Colin with a smile.

Ten miles away Keily Blurgh, the TV comedienne, was driving along winding country lanes with no idea where she was aiming for.

"What are you *doing*, girl?" she asked herself.

Kate and Form scurried along the corridor, both adjusting their clothing and discussing the best course of action, when they bumped into Maybelline coming the other way, looking rather lost.

"Maybelline!" cried Kate.

Form was slightly star-struck for a moment. He coughed. "Maybelline," he said holding his hand forward to shake her hand.

"Hello!" she replied and shook his hand

Form laughed awkwardly. "You don't know who I am!"

Maybelline laughed. "Isn't that supposed to be my line?"

Kate snorted quite unbecomingly. "We know who you are."

Form gave her a withering look.

Colin and Romme stood steadfast as the wind from the helicopter swept the lawn as it landed. As soon as the helicopter came to a halt the door opened and two very large men jumped out, closely followed by Chardonnay Blythe, the wife of the prime minister.

Chardonnay hit the ground running as usual. She briskly walked forward, offered her hand to Romme and Colin to shake and let them introduce themselves.

"Well, Colin," she began while walking at a brisk pace towards the house. "We have a lot to do. Obviously security is going to be very important. These are two of my men. We have decided the best option is to set up some sort of spurious road blocks. Apparently we can manage with just two positioned about half a mile in either direction from the main gates which is handy."

Colin nodded vigorously at each of her comments. Isn't she amazing, he thought with a sigh.

"We will have the road blocks in place within the next twenty minutes, I should think," she continued. "There is a rear entrance to the estate from a small access road. It will probably be best to bring any other visitors in that way, I think. I don't want to appear rude, but can I delay the introductions to everyone for the moment. I imagine you have an office with security cameras and a computer somewhere. That is probably where I should be for now."

Romme groaned. Colin gave him a stern glance.

"My office is a mess," whispered Romme to Colin.

Colin raised his eyebrows and gave Romme another stern look.

"I won't be checking on your housekeeping abilities, Romme," said Chardonnay

Colin gave her an adoring look.

Romme raced on ahead to clear the magazines and empty crisp packets from his desk.

chapter twenty

Keily was beginning to get slightly panicked. Unquestioning following of instincts was not usually her style. She liked to know the score and right now she didn't even know where she was. But at least it was getting light now, she felt she was getting near, near what she wasn't sure, and she wasn't too sure she wanted to be that near to whatever it might be. Lots of comedians end up going loopy, maybe that's it, maybe this is the dive into madness, maybe I'm gonna think I'm Cleopatra by lunch time, she pondered. Suddenly she was brought from her reverie by two big black vans in the middle of the road.

Keily sat nervously waiting as one of the men from the van made his way towards her.

"Hello, Ms Blurgh," he said.

She nodded at him.

"We have orders to guide you to the house."

"Me?" she asked.

"Yes, Ms Blurgh, we are from Downing Street security, if you could just follow us." He flashed her an ID card and turned away. The vans moved giving her space to get through and a car on the other side made its way up a side road. An arm came out of the window and indicated for Keily to follow.

Keily blindly followed, muttering to herself, "What do you think you're doing, girl, this is the point in every movie where you usually say, run, run like the wind!"

The car pulled over. Keily pulled in behind it, put on her central locking, then took it off, then put it on again and rolled down the window.

"What are we doing stopping here?" she asked, a tremor in her voice.

"I do apologise for the inconvenience, Ms Blurgh," said the security man, "We have instructions to bring you here. You will be met by someone from the house. I'm afraid you have to go through the stile over there." He pointed. "We have been told to park your car further down." He held his hand out to her, indicating he expected her to get out of her car.

He thinks I know why I'm here, she thought to herself!

Maybelline had positioned herself at the kitchen table and was instructing Tinny on her and Greg's special dietary needs. Form and Alison were huddled in the corner whispering about Chardonnay's arrival. Form pondered if he should go and introduce himself or leave her to get on with things. Alison had informed him of how Chardonnay had apparently taken charge of security. (Form could tell that for some reason Alison wasn't overly impressed by the Prime Minister's wife). He was quite surprised that Colin had handed over control so easily. He shrugged. Colin must have confidence in her; he always seemed to know what to do.

Kate sat amazed at the hustle and bustle of the kitchen, things going on as normal, housemaids running backwards and forwards, Tinny cooking for the five thousand by the looks of it, normal, normal, normal, and a space ship upstairs sending out signals to God knows where.

A rather shaky Keily stood at the side of the stile looking across the field towards the house.

"So, you're standing in a field at the break of dawn and you've just let someone drive off in your car and leave you here! Good thinking, girl," she said to herself.

She stiffened as she saw Romme making his way towards her in a golf cart. "Now you've got a gorilla in a milk float coming at you!"

Romme made a quick introduction of himself and put his hand up to assist Keily over the stile. She wobbled unsteadily as she put her leg over it. Romme lurched forward to steady her, but the ground was muddy. He slipped and pulled her over the stile and to the floor with him in one swift move.

"What the f**k!" screeched Keily.

Romme scrambled to his feet apologising profusely and attempting to wipe mud from Keily's clothes.

"Get off!" she shrugged at him. "This is f**kin' typical. Look at me! What the f**k is this all about?"

"Are you hurt?" asked Romme.

"No, no no, just tell me what this is all about, will you!" Keily's face was almost purple and she looked ready to burst.

"Well, I'm afraid that I'm just a monkey, Ms Blurgh, you'll have to speak to the organ grinder to know that, but I can tell you that we've had a lot of famous visitors today so you're in good company. Here let me help you." He guided her into the golf cart.

Keily composed herself and took a deep breath.

"Really? Who?" she asked.

Leo paced up and down by the door of the lab. Ned, Greg and Roger were accumulating another array of gadgets that Roger had deemed essentially required in the conservatory. Greg was itching to get up there and have a look, just as much as Ned and Leo were itching to show him.

Leo opened the conservatory door and with a flourish flung himself into the air. Greg was suitably impressed.

"Oh my f**king God!" he gasped

"Look at you, look at you!" he exclaimed pointing at Leo.

"I know," nodded Leo. "How cool is this?"

"Tres cool man, very tres cool," and he leaned into the air and bathed himself in the pink mist, luxuriating in it. He rolled around and then noticed his feet were not touching the ground.

He gave a short nervous giggle, nodded his head, "This is so cool."

In the office Chardonnay had efficiently set up communications with her 'men' on road blocks and was giving instructions to them frequently. Colin hovered around trying to anticipate her needs. His phone rang and he took the call in hushed tones so as not to disturb her.

"Well, Colin, we seem to be as ready as we can be for the moment," she sighed as she spun around in the chair to face him.

"I've just received a call from Professor Herring, ma'am, he's on his way via helicopter. He should be here within the hour."

Chardonnay nodded and considered this information. "Well, that is not an irregular occurrence here, is it?"

"No, ma'am, he is here frequently, and usually arrives via helicopter."

"That's fine then, no need to worry about the familiar!"

She's so calm, Colin thought. So in control, what a woman.

"Indeed, ma'am, Ms Blurgh will be here momentarily."

"Wonderful, I can't wait to meet her. She's a very funny lady. We all love Bonjella," she laughed mentally recalling Keily's character.

The white limousine, hardly an inconspicuous vehicle even in central London, made its way along the winding country roads, the occasional milk tanker and tractor the only other vehicles they had seen for miles. "Yes, yes, yes, this is the right road!" Eric said dismissively to the driver waving his hand indicating to the driver to carry on.

An unlikely trio indeed in the rear of the car. Eric Ipod, overtly camp, transvestite comedian and sometime people's poet, Cindy Ozzerly, wife and manager of wild man of rock, Olly Ozzerly and Cassy Chapel, child prodigy, voice of an angel, sang for the Pope when she was only ten, recently taken steps to replace her sweet little girl image with that of an all bumping, all grinding, all woman rock singer.

They had all been asked to be judges on a TV talent show the night before. Having sparked up immediate unexplained and unlikely bonds they had spent the whole night chatting and playing silly board games in Eric's hotel suite. They had unanimously and simultaneously decided they needed to go... somewhere, at 3am this morning and so here they were!

Keily walked into the office almost apologetically. Awkwardly she turned to Chardonnay and half bobbed as she shook hands.

"I'm so pleased to meet you, Keily, we just love your show. Can't wait to tell the kids I've met you," Chardonnay gushed.

Keily, rather taken aback by Chardonnay's enthusiastic welcome, flustered and fell into her best loved character, Bonjella.

"Well, bluddy gud to meet you's too. Gotta fag?"

Romme and Colin giggled. Chardonnay guffawed.

An embarrassed discussion of how Keily became covered in mud ensued. A bit of a wash and brush up before going to the lab was decided on as the best course of action.

Romme ducked under the helicopter blades and assisted the professor out and into his wheelchair before the blades had even slowed. Men on a mission, they made their way full speed to Romme's office as it had the easiest entrance. Romme excitedly told Samuel about the different celebrity presences, emphasising that Chardonnay was using his office. Samuel was not one to be easily impressed, and just nodded, acknowledging Romme's news.

"Yes, very good Romme, but I need to get to the lab right away, I can't be faffing around chatting. I have things to do."

Romme pulled a face and guided Samuel to the ramp entrance to his office.

Chardonnay rose to greet Samuel. He politely shook her hand.

"Yes, hello, very nice to meet you, but I must get on," he said abruptly and manoeuvred his chair to the interior door and left.

Chardonnay was slightly nonplussed by this. She looked at Romme who shrugged his shoulders and raised his eyes, indicating to Chardonnay that this wasn't unusual behaviour for the professor.

Chardonnay's phone rang and one of her men informed her of the approach of a white limousine.

"Yes, that's one of ours, show them through," she told him.

"How do you know?" asked Colin.

She shrugged. "I just do," she replied.

Colin understood. Having been a host he knew about suddenly just 'knowing' something with no explanation as to why.

As Colin left the office he bumped into Amy in the corridor.

"What are you doing here, girl?" he asked.

"Just on my way to the kitchen," she replied.

"No need for you to be here, Amy, get on with your work. We have a busy day ahead. No time for wandering aimlessly around! Come on, I'm going to the kitchen myself."

Ned, Leo and Greg all introduced themselves to Samuel with some deference. He attempted some polite introductions, but was totally distracted by the phenomenon that was occurring in the conservatory. With some difficulty straining against the thick, misty air, he made his way in his wheelchair to the table covered with gadgets that Roger was poring over and immediately was absorbed with readings that obviously amazed and astounded him and Roger alike.

After a moment of slight indignation at this rebuff, Ned, Leo and Greg returned to the serious business of perfecting their 'art' of floating. The rather ungainly frog manoeuvre they adopted had already been found to be the most effective.

As they made their way back to the conservatory Form and Kate quizzed Maybelline about her experience of being a host. She enthused much about the just 'knowing' and the feeling of total confidence she had gained suddenly, how every move in her career seemed obvious and worked out, and how she wasn't really aware of being a host at all. She laughed. "It's very clear now, but then I just thought the Muse had hit me!"

"Well, that's more or less what had happened, isn't it," countered Form.

They continued down the maze of corridors discussing the possibility of the aliens being the original Muses.

James perked as he watched the white limousine pass through the village, huddled in his car on the parking lot outside the post office. Grabbing his phone he texted a message excitedly.

chapter twenty-one

"Listen here, dear man," gushed Eric, "we have no idea what's going on. Do you think you could make things clearer?"

He beckoned the policeman toward the open rear door of the limo he was standing beside.

Cindy popped her head out of the door. "What's the problem?"

The policeman spun on his heel and pulled a face towards his colleagues in the van. "Cindy Ozzerly, woo hoo!" He mouthed to them.

"Hello, sir, madam," he nodded at Cindy and addressed himself to Eric. "We are from Downing Street security. We understand you are visiting the Stygbee estate, sir?"

"Is that right?" Eric aimed his enquiry at Cindy.

"Yes, yes that's it. What security firm did you say you were?"

"No madam, sorry, you misunderstood, we are from the security offices at Downing Street."

"Ooooooooooo," piped in Eric raising his eyebrows and placing his hands on his hips. "Best no argue with you guys then!"

"Did you intend to?" asked the policeman.

Cindy laughed and turned into the car to relay the information that this all seemed to be government shit. "Got Tony's men looking after us no less!" to Cassy sitting in the car.

"Such nice suits," said Eric running his hand down the arm of the policeman's jacket. "Armani?"

"Yes, thank you," he replied distancing himself from Eric who gave a wry smile.

"Oh, don't wind him up, Eric, he's gotta guide us gently up this back passage," laughed Cindy.

"Just commenting on the marvellous fashion sense of our gorgeous forces men, deary. We place ourselves in your hands officer!" he finished with a wink and climbed back in the car. "Shove over, will you, how much space do you need for, God's sake?"

"Don't let Maybelline see me looking like this please," pleaded Keily to Colin as they made their way to the south wing.

"You can take one of the guest rooms along here if you like. I am assuming you might need a changes of clothes. Did you pack a bag when you came?"

Keily was embarrassed. "No, I didn't, God, I'm daft, I just came," she finished, looking at him feebly.

"Not to worry," he said as he guided her towards one of the big oak panelled doors. "This room should be fine. There are robes in the bathroom. I will send up some clothes."

"Just a pair of joggers and a sweatshirt would be fine. I'm not fussy."

"Well, we can manage that but I can send up a selection of items for you to select, perhaps some jeans and some T-shirts. We have a whole cupboard of T-shirts from every band that's ever recorded here."

"Oh right, well, that would be lovely."

"Would you like something to eat as well? I can send something up when they bring the clothes."

"Well, actually," she laughed, "I'm starving. I'd kill for a cup of tea, well, a *big* mug," she joked.

"Can I suggest some bacon sandwiches?"

"Oh, you read my mind, that would be wonderful. Aww you're really lovely you are," she leant forward and gently punched his arm.

"It's a delight. I think you are an amazing comedienne. You have already given me so much pleasure."

Keily turned away in a coy manner. "Aww, don't you embarrass me."

"Indeed, but I speak the truth." He left Keily to wander round the bedroom trying not to touch anything with her muddy hands but wanting to have a nose round at the same time.

Romme came speeding towards the stile with a large security man and two bales of straw aboard.

"Oh my good God, what's this?" exclaimed Cindy.

"Two grizzly bears making a getaway with a new bed?" Chipped in Eric.

They all stood by the sty giggling at the sight approaching them. As Romme pulled up the security man jumped out, and made straight off down the road without even acknowledging them. Romme began frantically spreading straw over the large mud puddle. "I do apologise, I will be with you in just one second."

"Are we going in that milk cart?" asked Cassy.

"It won't be my first time on a milk cart, I can tell you," leered Eric.

Cassy jabbed him with her elbow. "Will we all fit on? Or do we have to make two trips?"

"I don't mind squashing up if you don't," returned Eric.

"I always enjoy a good squash with you, Eric," said Cindy taking his arm and squeezing him.

"Get off me, you insatiable creature. You're a married woman, and your handbag doesn't match your shoes, get off," he said pushing her away.

"You know you love me really," she crooned adopting a 'baby' voice.

"Yes, well, you know her bag would have matched her shoes, IF she didn't have to go and get a bigger one to hold all your rubbish!" countered Cassy, wagging her head at Eric.

"RUBBISH! RUBBISH! Designer rubbish I'll have you know!"

Romme stood at the other side of the stile waiting to give assistance over it. "The cart does seat four people. Would you like to come this way?" He held out his hand towards Cassy who was closest.

As Maybelline entered the conservatory Greg rushed at her, picking her up and twirling her around seemingly in slow motion as he fought against the thick air. "This is *such* an adventure," he held her to him closely. "Mmm, I'm so glad you're here too. You won't believe this stuff," he finished spinning her towards the chimney breast.

Alison made straight for Samuel and began hurriedly whispering to him. Roger listened in nodding as she told them about the other arrivals and arrangements that were being made.

"Do you know who else is here, do you?" chirped in Kate excitedly, skipping over clapping her hands like an excited child towards Leo and Ned.

"Alllllll right, our kid," said Leo in an exaggerated drawl to Maybelline.

"Someone else arrived then?" asked Greg.

"This is *amazing,*" said Maybelline moving around the conservatory coating herself in the waves and gazing upwards to take in the dome.

"Oh, you better believe it, honey, *this* is *some* trip," Ned told her; he put his arm around her affectionately like a familiar friend and guided her to look at the sphere.

"I have to go," Alison announced. "Staff morning meeting." She shrugged, nodded to Kate and Maybelline and hurried out.

"OK, ta ta, Alison," Maybelline pulled herself from her reverie to call after Alison as she made off down the stairway.

Greg walked up beside Maybelline as she and Ned stood gazing at the oyster, put his arm around her waist and put his head on her shoulder, his hand stroking her tummy.

"Mmm, Mrs Rigsby, Mr Snuggly wants to play!"

Leo and Kate raised their eyebrows at each other then shrugged and moved over to join the others, standing staring.

"Mr Snuggly always wants to play," laughed Maybelline.

"Any chance of getting some privacy in here?" said Greg loudly.

Maybelline gave him a playful punch. "Get your brain out of your trousers, Mister!"

"But May!" he exclaimed in a childish whinge.

Ned leaned over to Kate, "Can't blame him, that machine leaves ya feeling right horny!"

"I get the feeling that it don't take much to get *him* horny," countered Kate.

"Bloody ages since I felt horny," mumbled Roger absentmindedly.

Ned and Kate exchanged wry smiles.

"As you know, the engagement party is tonight. We all have lots of work to do, as usual," Colin said to his staff as he walked along the line checking their uniforms. "We have some very important people coming."

Amy piped in, "Maybelline's here, isn't she? Will we be able to get autographs?" She was obviously excited about the potential for celebrity meetings. She was prone to being starstruck; on meeting Supergrass a few weeks ago, she had been so excited that when she met them she had opened her mouth to speak to the lead singer, and just burped, right into his face! She had been mortified!

"Amy, my dear," said Colin scanning the others to check they were all listening to him.

"Our guests are not to be bothered by *anyone* until after the party." They met this with shuffled nods of understanding.

"The south wing is out of bounds unless given specific instruction, OK? Mr James is to be kept away from the south wing also. I don't imagine he will be wanting to go there, but keep an eye out and keep him busy if you get the opportunity. I don't want it to be obvious we are keeping him away though. The stage is being set up in the garden, also we have the flowers and exterior decorations arriving."

Alison strode into the kitchen. "Yes, and you two," she said pointing to two of the maids, "I want you to make up the favours, please, guest room 5 needs to be redone. Amy, you can do that after you've finished Mr Form's and Miss Kate's rooms."

"Do you want me to refresh the linens in the south wing rooms?" Amy asked.

"Amy!" Alison replied sharply. "You will *all* behave in an efficient professional manner, this is the ultimate test for us. You will be given your instructions, and I expect them to be carried out *to the letter*! Secrecy is the top priority, if we end up with paparazzi reporters storming the estate because *someone*," she looked directly at Amy, "texts all their friends to impress them, then *someone* will be hung drawn and quartered by *me*!"

Amy nodded. "Shall I put new linens in the south wing then?"

The other staff giggled.

Cindy, Eric and Cassy sat awkwardly squashed together on Romme's sofa, patiently waiting for Chardonnay to finish talking on the phone to her security men.

"I feel like I'm sitting outside the headmaster's office at school," whispered Eric to Cindy.

"I've decided I'm a secret agent waiting for my debriefing on my mission!" she replied.

"Dun dun der da dun dun," Eric hummed the Mission Impossible theme tune and turned to Cassy pointing his fingers at her as if holding a gun.

Cassy laughed. "I'm supposed to be the kid here, you know!"

Eric slid off the sofa and rolled on the floor, springing up and pointing his 'gun' at them both. "I'm Bond... Basildon Bond!"

"Oh, you'd make a great secret agent, Eric," said Chardonnay rising from the desk and walking towards them holding out her hand in greeting. "You're so inconspicuous!" she said with a twinkle in her eye.

Cindy laughed. "Don't know about the elusive Pimpernel, more like pimple on the bum!"

Cassy stood up as Chardonnay offered her hand in greeting. "*You* know what's happening here, don't you? We have no idea why we are here!"

Chardonnay nodded.

Cindy interrupted Cassy. "Yes, we're just winging it here. It's weird coz I always need to know what's happening but this morning I just felt." She paused.

"Guided," interjected Cassy.

"Yes, guided," agreed Cindy. "Seeing you here, Mrs Blythe."

"Chardonnay, please call me Chardonnay."

"Oh OK, Chardonnay, well, seeing you here is a bit worrying. Are we involved in some government plot?"

Eric clapped his hands together. "Please say yes! I always wanted to have a secret identity and a pen that shoots tranquilliser darts!"

Keily sat on the edge of the bed in a fluffy white robe, looking lost and obviously waiting.

Amy knocked and entered pushing a trolley which had Keily's breakfast on it and underneath held a pile of clothes.

"Oh wonderful," exclaimed Keily.

"Hello, Ms Blurgh," Amy stuttered.

"I am *so* hungry."

Amy smiled. "I am instructed to show you to the south wing once you have eaten and changed. There is a selection of clothes here for you to choose from."

"Excellent, excellent," said Keily picking up a sandwich from the trolley and leaning down to look at the clothes.

"If I lay the clothes out on the bed for you, Ms Blurgh, you can choose easier."

"OK, yes, good idea, Batman," Keily said with a mouth full of bacon sandwich. "So, who's in the south wing then?"

Amy perked. "Maybelline!" she exclaimed.

"Have you seen her?" asked Keily.

"No, not yet."

"I'm wondering what she's wearing. I don't want to look smeggy when I meet Maybelline, do I?"

"Well, you can't look worse than me! I hate this uniform."

Keily smiled. "Believe me, I can! Bonjella's sense of style was based on my own," she said.

Amy laughed. "Well, let's find you something stylish from this lot then." She paused. "I knew you were going to be lovely." she said.

"You're lucky you came armed with food," Keily quipped and taking a stance did an Incredible Hulk impression. "Don't leave me hungry, you wouldn't like me when I'm hungry."

Amy chuckled. "A bacon sarnie saved my life."

Form held a phone to his ear and held his other arm out waving to Kate to come closer. "I'm going to call James and send him to London on an errand. What kind of errand do you recommend?"

"Don't let him take the helicopter. Say you need to use it."

"What for?"

"I don't know. He's your servant he shouldn't ask questions!"

"He's not a servant. Don't call him that."

Kate gave Form a withering look. "Oh, do shut up, Form, you know what I meant."

"So?" asked Form.

"What?" replied Kate.

"So, what do I send him to London for?"

Maybelline interjected. "Kate, you're so slow off the mark here! I'd be suggesting a trip to Tiffany's if I were you, girlfriend!"

They all laughed.

"Tiffany's it is then," said Form.

Maybelline gave Kate a wink, Kate grinned widely.

"Anybody else starving?" asked Greg.

Samuel suggested that it would be a good idea to make their way to the laboratory 'lounge' to wait in comfort for the others and get a cup of tea.

"Sounds good to me," said Greg. He wrapped his arms around Maybelline and whispered in her ear, "We gotta get private in here, hunnie." She turned to him, smiled seductively and winked.

Ned smooched up to Greg. "I know where you're coming from man. If I stay here much longer, even Roger's gonna start looking attractive!"

"Too right, bro," Leo responded. "This place feels like the right place for a flipping orgy, sexual energy flying round. Anyone wanna get all Roman?" he laughed.

"Where's the groupies when you need them, eh, bro?" said Ned.

Form visibly tensed. "I really don't think that's a very good idea. We have Chardonnay Blythe in the house, you know!"

"Cor, I bet she's a go'er," responded Leo.

Form's face reddened. "I do hope you are joking. That's hardly an appropriate way to speak of the wife of our Prime Minister!"

"I ain't joking. Tony always seems to be smiling"

"She's got legs that go right up to her arse," interjected Greg.

Maybelline Guffawed!

chapter twenty-two

The high pitched screech Eric gave out made everyone at the table jump and turn to the door as he, Cindy and Cassy entered the lab. He dashed towards Maybelline and the room echoed with mwah mwah kisses.

Leo stood up, hips dropped and arms fell open wide. "Hey, Cassy," he drawled.

Excited friendly banter flew around. Eric made much of saying that he knew Ned and Leo had to be aliens all along. "Two ugly bast**ds like you couldn't possibly have thought you'd get away with it otherwise!"

"Voice of an angel me, man, voice of an angel," swaggered Leo in response.

"Only angelic thing about you though!" quipped Cindy.

"Aww, Cindy, don't believe all you read about me in the papers. I'm a pussycat," he whined as he wrapped his arms around her.

"I sent most of those stories in, honey," she laughed.

"Hello, James, I've been trying to get hold of you," said Form into the old black bakelite telephone on the desk.

"Yes, yes, very early, I've had a thought, I need you to pop to London for me!"

Kate leant over Form's shoulder and mimed putting rings on her fingers. He smiled.

"You're where? Oh really, well I'd rather you went straight to London…Yes, I can see that, well, see you soon then." Form gave Kate a withered look. "He's already almost here. We can pack him back off to London in ten minutes, no worries!"

Kate didn't look so sure.

In the office Chardonnay took the call from the heliport, requesting permission to land. Hearing the name of the passenger Chardonnay approved permission immediately and then excitedly called her 'men' and told them to dismantle the road block.

"Job done, boys, you can pack up and go home."

Ray Warbler fidgeted in the seat of the helicopter.

"We got the OK to land, cool, I knew we would."

He clapped his hands excitedly like a little boy and craned his head to look out of the window, pressing his nose on it endeavouring to see the ground below.

"How far now? Long? How far?"

Colin received a call from Chardonnay letting him know of Ray's imminent appearance.

"Oh no, we can't let him bump into James!" said Form.

"We'll meet James out front," said Kate already making her way to the door.

"Yes, and Colin, you meet Ray and scoot him up here ASAP."

"Ray's here!!" squealed Cassy.

Ned and Leo didn't look quite so pleased.

"Is that all of us?" asked Maybelline.

"I reckon," said Ned.

"Me too," nodded Greg.

Tom shook his head. "Ray Warbler, blimey."

Having run through the house, taking a detour into the study to pick up the diary James had said he needed, Kate decided her skills were better used meeting Ray! Form was unsure if her reason was entirely a practical one. Form was flushed-faced and out of breath as he ran down the entrance steps to meet James, whose attention had already been caught by the arrival of the helicopter. He was already wandering inquisitively towards the gardens. Form called out and gestured James toward him. Reluctantly James turned to Form.

"Here's your diary," Form offered.

James absently reached for the proffered diary. "Who's arriving?"

"I'm not sure, Samuel I think. Listen James, I've realised that Kate needs some jewellery for the party, you know something special that shows off her status!" Form finished. As he turned from James he chastised himself. Status, what was he thinking? And shook his head.

"Good idea. Shall I get Harvey Nick's to send up a selection for you to choose from?"

"No!" Form blurted out. He coughed. "I mean, no, I would prefer if you picked a selection. I mean, you know Kate, and you've got good taste and you will know what she should have, not some sales girl who has no idea."

"We can take a look online in my office, and pick out a few pieces," suggested James.

"Ah! Yes, good idea, James," Form cringed.

James was still looking toward the helicopter, craning to see who emerged. He suddenly lurched forward waving his hand in the air. "Ray!" he called. "It's Ray, Ray Warbler, you know him, don't you?" James directed toward Form.

"Is it? Wow!" said Form. "Ray Warbler eh! Fancy that."

"You'll like him, he's a nice bloke. I've met him a few times," James called back to Form as he made his way at some speed over to meet Ray.

Reluctantly Form followed. This was not going to plan. Although he had to admit as plans go, it hadn't been the best one ever.

Ray obviously recognised James and waved to him as he exited the helicopter.

Colin and Kate cringed as they followed Ray's eye line and caught a glimpse of James coming round the hedges closely followed by Form.

"Well done, Form," mumbled Kate. Colin grimaced.

"Way hey, Jamie me ol mucker," exclaimed Ray striding toward him, Colin and Kate scurrying quite ungraciously behind.

"Mr Warbler, sir, Mr Warbler, sir," Colin called, his breath laboured as the helicopter blades restarted and he and Kate ran into the gusts of wind it created. Kate held on tightly to the hem of her skirt, not the most glamorous of looks.

As Keily tentatively put her head round the door to peer down the long corridor Amy was making her way along the corridor holding a pile of nice crisp sheets.

"Hello," Amy said brightly.

"Hello," returned Keily. "I'm not sure what I'm supposed to be doing. I think I should find Colin. Do you know where he is?"

"Well, not right at this minute I don't know where he is, but he's been in the laboratory on and off this morning. Shall I take you there?"

Keily wasn't too sure she wanted to go to a laboratory. She still didn't trust these feelings 100%. As usual her vivid imagination kicked in and she saw images of Frankenstein's monster being created, her head on the body of the current women's shot putt champion!

Amy leaned into Keily in a conspiratorial manner. "I'm not supposed to say anything," she whispered. "But I guess it's OK to tell you, coz you're here, and you're already famous."

Keily nodded. "Yes, yes, I am."

"Well, do you know who's already in the lab?"

"No, who?"

Amy held herself up tall and proudly announced, "Maybelline an' her husband the film bloke, Leo an' Ned from

Pond Life, Pond Life!" Her voice took on a tone of incredulity. "Cassy Chapel, Eric Ipod *and* Cindy Ozzerly!"

"Wow, that's some company!" Keily said with a smile. Amy's excitement was very charming, she thought.

"Can I show you the way?" Amy pleaded. "I'm not really allowed up there coz I texted my mate once before when Supergrass were here, and now they don't trust me, but I really wouldn't do anything stupid, I promise!"

"Lead the way, Amy, let's see if we can get you some autographs!"

"And yours, can I have yours too?" Amy enthusiastically asked.

Everyone stood to greet Chardonnay as she entered the lab, and bombarded her with questions.

"Hold on, hold on," she said. "I'm sorry but I only have the same answers as you do."

"Oh, come off it, Chardonnay," whined Eric. "Wife of the prime minister knows everything."

"Not when it's concerning aliens I'm afraid, Eric. Ask me about the plans for cycle routes through Bermondsey and I might be able to help you."

"Can you let us know anything about plans to pelt the Tory leader with kippers?" limply joked Eric, nervous suddenly and unsure why.

"Oh shut up, you fool," interjected Cassy.

"Shut up yourself," Eric replied.

"I hear Ray's here," mumbled Leo.

"Yes, that's all of us I think. Now time for some answers for us all," said Chardonnay.

"You're gonna have to let this drop," whispered Cindy to Leo.

"Oh, he just gets on my tits, Cindy. Thinks the sun comes up just to hear him crow, he does."

"Yeah, well, you ain't exactly Mr Modesty yourself are you? Give it a rest. It's only coz you're so alike. The three of you could be brothers for f**ks sake, like bloody triplets."

Leo put his hand out to Cindy. "Wotever," and walked away.

Ned put his arm around Cindy's shoulder. "Take no notice of him, he'll come round, likes to throw his rattle outa the pram now and again. He hasn't done it for at least three hours so it's due."

As they made their way through the house towards the recording studio James and Ray were imbibed in cheerful conversation, reminiscing about an apparently very exciting week that Ray had spent at the house about five years earlier, just before he had launched his solo career.

Colin broke away from them and made his way toward his office as they climbed the stairway and along the corridor to the south wing, Ray being swept along in conversation with James, Form and Kate scurrying behind them furtively trying to work out how they were going to distract James before they reached the lab. As they turned the corner Ray caught sight of Keily and Amy making their way from the west wing.

Ray put his fingers to his lips and let out a shrill whistle. "Hey!" he shouted and waved to Keily. She gave an excited squeaky "Hi" and stiffly raised her hand in a waving motion.

Kate tapped Form on the arm, smiled and whispered, "Don't worry. I've got this now." She sidled over so she stood just slightly behind James, and then almost leaning over him she pointed a finger at Amy.

"Amy! What are you doing? I know you're not supposed to be here!" she said quite angrily. Everyone turned to look at her and then at Amy who was holding her pile of sheets in front of her like a shield.

James visibly stiffened and took an authoritative step forward. James was well aware of Amy's 'banned' status from anything one didn't want bandied about. He had dealt with the fall out from her indiscretions before. He turned to Ray. "Lovely to see you again, I'll join you later. I hope you don't mind if I leave you here, but this is a staff issue I have to deal with."

"No problem, mate, business and all that, catch ya later."

Form and Kate smiled at each other as they made their introductions to Keily and led their guests to the lab.

James sharply told Amy to follow him "Now!"

Eric gently took Chardonnay's hand and whispered to her, "Come with me, let me show it to you," and led her out of the lab. All the others seemed to be hugely tired and were sluggishly trying to create comfortable places to catch five minutes' kip and paid no attention to Eric and Chardonnay's departure.

"Is it calling you as loudly as it's calling me?" he asked.

"Only since you took my hand," she replied.

Mouths wide open they entered the conservatory, heavily leaning against the wispy pink air. They uncertainly made their way into the room, turning around, soaking up the atmosphere, smiling and reassuringly nodding at each other.

Eric caught sight of the sphere and froze. Chardonnay's eyes followed his glance. She gasped, "Blimey."

Eric walked forward attempting to hasten his speed by parting the air with his hands "It's like walking through candyfloss without the stickiness."

Chardonnay leant forward, a little more, a little more "Eric!" she shrieked. "I'm floating, look, look, look, Eric look!"

"No, shit, Sherlock, look at you!" Eric leant forward into the same position Chardonnay was awkwardly 'hanging' in the air. "Woo hoo," he whooped!

With a rather clumsy wading gait they made their way closer to the sphere, huffing and puffing at the energy required to move forward.

"Floating on music," Chardonnay mused to herself.

"It sounds so far away though, doesn't it? Do you know the music? I feel I do, but I couldn't tell you what it is," Eric mumbled as he relaxed into his floating.

They looked at each other as they approached the sphere and tentatively put their hands out to touch it.

Samuel, Roger and Tom huddled together over their machines and talked excitedly in hushed whispers as all around the lab lay the snoozing bodies of Ned, Leo, Cassy, Cindy, Maybelline and Greg.

Ray and Keily, arm in arm, made their way along the corridor chatting like a couple who had known each other years.

As Eric and Chardonnay touched the sphere it vibrated with a large hum. Eric and Chardonnay shuddered.

The sleeping bodies in the lab shuddered and continued sleeping.

Ray and Keily shuddered and continued walking.

James and Amy shuddered and smiled!

As Eric and Chardonnay slid cautiously into the sphere, the humming vibration increased. They clutched each other's hands and gave an excited squeeze, as the sphere rose sharply.

Ray giggled like a schoolboy when he entered the lab and was faced with the vision of slumbering bodies. He raised his finger to his lips and tiptoed in, Keily, Form and Kate following behind him mimicking his moves. A simultaneous "Whoa" erupted from the sleepers, Ray and Keily as they all lurched as if hit by some aftershock that Form, Kate, Tom, Roger and Samuel did not seem to feel.

Lightly Eric launched himself out of the sphere as it softly returned to the ground and bobbed gently to standing position. Chardonnay lay back and floated for a moment.

"Well, that's made everything so much clearer," said Chardonnay with a sigh.

"What a trip, *what a trip,*" Eric mused. "I feel pretty, oh so pretty, I feel pretty and witty and bright." He began to sing with wide grandiose gestures twirling and spinning as he floated about six inches off the ground.

Ray and Keily's arrival was greeted with forced enthusiasm from Maybelline, Greg, Ned, Leo, Cindy and Cassy who all seemed to be exhausted. Roger and Tom took them both in hand and endeavoured to put them in the picture as much as they could. Keily stayed close to Ray, shyly using him as a screen. The conversation was punctuated with hushed 'wows' and 'reallys' from both Ray and Keily.

Maybelline and Greg sluggishly roused themselves and announced that they were going to catch an hour's comfortable sleep in the dormitory.

chapter twenty-three

"Is everything OK?" asked Maybelline of Chardonnay as they approached each other in the corridor outside the lab.

"Fine, fine, fine," Chardonnay assured her with a wide smile.

"We were going for a kip," said Greg. "I'm knackered," he continued with a drowsy yawn.

"Good idea," Eric said. "Probably a good idea for all of us to get some rest. We can't do anything much for a while, a few hours at least."

"How d'you know that?" Maybelline enquired.

"They just do, May, leave it at that, let's get some sleep," moaned Greg.

Eric gave a sympathetic nod towards the remaining slumberers. Chardonnay smiled and nodded. They enthusiastically greeted Ray and Keily. Eric and Ray knew each other from old and spent sometime enthusing about 'if only they had known'.

Chardonnay took an authoritative stance. "Eric, we have something we have to do, don't we. Form and Kate, we need a quiet word with you." She waved her hand toward the door. "Could you lead the way, Form, somewhere quiet, please."

Kate and Form exchanged inquisitive glances but did not question Chardonnay. They had learnt not to recently! Go with the flow was the best way just now.

Eric reluctantly followed them out.

Greg gave a groan of pleasure as he entered the conservatory, leaning lazily into the air. "Mmm, we can sleep here, like sleeping on clouds, angels sleeping on clouds, dreaming, sleeping, floating, mmm."

Maybelline followed him in luxuriating and floating. They wrapped themselves together and made their way to the sofa, invisible in the pink mist. The energy in the air stirred them. Maybelline groaned sensually. "Let's make love."

"I thought you'd never ask," laughed Greg grasping her tightly to him and kissing her passionately. Then he pushed her away, holding her lightly in the air, sliding his hands up her skirt and tugging her 'tummy tight' knickers off. She giggled. "Sexy big knickers, honey," and wiggled to help him remove them. Leaving her floating Greg slid down to her feet sliding her knickers off. Then kneeling on the sofa he cupped her buttocks in his hands and pulled her toward him. Her legs floating over his shoulders he passionately kissed her groin. Maybelline squealed in delight.

Form wandered randomly in the corridor, wondering which room to use. What did Eric and Chardonnay want? Would a dorm room do?

"Is this room OK," he asked opening a random door.

"Yes, fine," replied Chardonnay.

"I don't actually know what's in this room. I've only ever used the lab and the main dorm and the kitchen and the toilet, oh yes, and of course the conservatory on this wing. This house is like a maze, I was only used to a two bedroom flat before. Pretty difficult to get lost in a two bedroom flat," he gabbled.

"A sat nav sounds like a good idea," joked Eric.

"A ball of string is more Form's kind of technology, Eric," laughed Kate.

"I'll crack it yet," said Form. "It's like a taxi driver learning 'The Knowledge'. I'll have it all mapped in here within the month," he retorted, tapping his head.

"OK, I'll have the ball of string then," said Kate.

Form became serious again. "What do you need us to do?" he asked.

Eric and Chardonnay straightened themselves and stood facing Form and Kate.

"We have a gift for you both," said Chardonnay.

"I'm not sure I want to give it to you though," muttered Eric.

"Oh don't be so stupid," Chardonnay dismissively said.

"You don't need to give me anything, Eric. I have much more than I need, more things than I will ever use. If you want to keep whatever it is, you keep it, I'm fine, honestly," blurted Form.

"No, no, no, he's just being silly." Chardonnay turned to Eric. "It won't change things, you'll be fine, you won't even miss it, you know that."

"I know, I know," grumbled Eric like a naughty schoolboy who has just been told to share his sweets.

"We have to hand over our 'beings' to you," announced Chardonnay.

"Oh," was Form's response.

"Why us? Oh my God." Kate paused. "Blimey."

"We're just following instructions that we're not too sure we understand in the first place, winging it, playing by ear, same as all of us. It's this 'knowing' thing and not being able to explain! Eric blurted. "I know it sounds selfish but it's made me so much better. All the languages I can speak. I've written really good shows with this thing in me."

"It won't change, Eric," Chardonnay tried to reassure him.

"So you say, so you think, but you don't *know,* do you?"

"No, I don't, it's all a leap of faith now. I'm scared too, I didn't know I had it till last night but I'm scared I'm going to miss it. Colin's explained to me, once you are the best you can be, you can do the job, you don't lose any talents you've gained, just new ones have to be worked on at a normal pace." She put her arm around his shoulder. "It's OK, come on, let's get it done."

"Do you want to have a cup of coffee and a quiet moment beforehand?" asked Kate kindly.

Eric sat down on the edge of the bed. "Would that be OK?" he asked. "So much is happening so fast, my head needs a break."

"Good idea," said Chardonnay

"I'll go and get some," said Form already heading out of the door.

Naked and glistening with sweat Greg and Maybelline curled up together wrapped in the blanket on the sofa and slept, serene smiles across their faces, wrapped in the thick pink mist. Somewhere far off in the distance a sound, a giggle?

Eric lay down on the bed, Chardonnay sat herself in the armchair by the window and closed her eyes. Kate sat on the edge of the bed and stared blankly at the wall.

As Form re-entered the lab, Ned, Leo, Cindy and Cassy were all around the table squirming in the seats, resting their heads on the hard surface and generally looking very uncomfortable. He walked over and tapped Ned on the shoulder.

"There are dorm rooms all along the corridor, plenty of soft beds for you to take some rest in. I think you have a couple of hours if you need them."

Ned looked sleepily up at Form. "That sounds so cool, mate." He roused himself and to the others said, "Come on, let's get comfy." With muttered tired groans they followed him out, Cindy muttering to herself unsure as to why she felt so tired. "I feel like I've climbed a mountain!"

At the far end of the lab by the wind turbine machine Ray and Keily were in deep conversation, Keily slightly taken aback by Ray stroking her hair from her face.

Form collected some mugs together and washed them up as the kettle boiled. "Coffee, tea anyone?" he called.

Positive responses from everyone. Ray and Keily made their way toward Form.

Uncertainly Form turned to Ray and Keily. "Eric and Chardonnay are going to give me and Kate their 'beings'!" He waited for their response.

Keily shrugged, "Don't ask me, I'm new to all this, I went to visit Reggie Howler last Wednesday." She became sad. "He was a great friend and mentor to me. I'm so glad I got to see him before he went."

Reggie Howler was an institution in English comedy and had died only days earlier.

"He held me close and I felt something like an electric shock, no, nicer than that, a rush." She looked at Ray who nodded his understanding. "I thought it was some kind of 'near death' type thingy."

"Well, you would," piped in Form.

"I went home and wrote a whole TV series! Just like that… Poof and it was done."

"It was the same for me, rattled off a whole album in three days from blank page to finished master tape!" declared Ray with a laugh. "I thought I was *so* talented."

"You are," said Keily.

"With a little help from alien beings I am," he replied.

Ned tapped on the door of Cindy's chosen room, and he tentatively popped his head around the door. "Cindy, Cindy, fancy a cuddle?"

Cindy responded only to open the quilt to allow Ned to join her in the bed.

Leo lay in his bed texting messages and jokes to Cassy. He could hear her giggling in the next room.

"You should go up and take a look at the sphere. I'm surprised no one has taken you up there already," Form said to Ray and Keily as he left the lab holding a tray of coffee.

Tom perked. "Yes, yes, you must see the conservatory. It's just... Wow, I'll show you!"

"Take them up there and collect that tachograph reading while you're there. Bring it straight back here," boomed Roger.

Tom led Ray and Keily to the conservatory eagerly telling them what they were in store for.

"Floating! No!" said Ray. "You're having me on!"

May and Greg roused as they heard Tom enter the conservatory with a loud "Da Daaa!" Greg placed his hand over May's mouth. They giggled conspiratorially and scanned around for their clothes lost in the thick pink mist.

Ray and Keily were suitably astounded by the vision before them, wading through the air with mouths hanging open. Tom launched himself at the air and gently floated to the floor.

"You can do it better than me, you've got the 'beings'. Ned and Leo were sort of almost flying!"

"I'm tingling all over, this is amazing," whispered Keily.

"Want to learn to fly, fair maiden?" asked Ray.

"Fair maiden, my arse," replied Keily.

"And a fair arse too, I have no doubt," he returned.

"Fair? It's more than fair, it's white, like a beautiful lump of fresh clean lard!" she laughed.

Tom laughed heartily. "You crack me up you do," he said to Keily.

"Ta," she replied.

Ray launched himself confidently into the air. "It's like crowd surfing, without the hands and beer bottles."

Keily joined him, if slightly less confidently.

"There, you're getting the hang of it," commented Tom. He made his way to the machine taking readings on the table as Ray and Keily were drawn toward the sphere. He made a great play of running but going nowhere. They reached out to stroke it, and the sphere gave a deep hum again. Ray shuddered, Keily shuddered. Greg and May shuddered. Tom collated his numbers.

"I've gotta get back to the prof. You two wanna stay here a bit longer, I s'pose?"

They nodded remaining mesmerised by the sphere and the atmosphere, coating themselves in it. Ray drew close behind Keily and whispered into her neck. "I am unbelievably horny. All I can think of is ripping your knickers off"

Keily laughed, embarrassed. "Don't be daft, it's not me! It's the aliens that are making you horny, not me!"

"It's you, Keily, believe me, it's you. I've always fancied you, you make me laugh, that twinkle in your eyes."

"Oh, do me a favour," Keily implored. "Ray, I'm not daft, you have super models falling at your feet, you don't want a lardy ugly bird, no matter how much she makes you laugh!"

"Oh, don't I?"

"No, you don't."

Ray grabbed Keily and enveloped her in a passionate kiss, sending them both floating through the air. They glanced off the top of the table and bobbed to the floor in a passionate clinch, pulling each other's clothes off, lips locked, thrusting against each other. Naked they caressed each other groaning loudly as they rolled on the misty floor.

Greg and Maybelline pulled embarrassed faces at each other and concentrated on gathering up their clothes as quickly and quietly as possible.

Ray and Keily found themselves floating in an upright position. Ray spun Keily round and bent her over the table. Taking her by the hips from behind they began to f**k like animals, grunting and groaning, Keily floating just above the table, her legs wrapped around the table legs to keep her still and give some purchase.

"Bloody hell," murmured Greg.

Eric, Chardonnay, Form and Kate stood in the dorm room all looking apprehensive.

"How does this work?" asked Form

"Let's just hold hands," suggested Chardonnay

As their hands connected Form and Kate shuddered. "Gosh!" exclaimed Kate.

"Oh my God, oh my God, oh my God," gasped Keily.

"Yes indeedy deedy do," sighed Ray.

"I can't believe we just did that."

"I wouldn't be surprised if they've got CCTV here, u wanna check? Or shall we have a replay?"

"Shut up, Ray! I'm serious, what was I thinking of, I don't do this sort of thing," she said suddenly panicking.

"Shut up worrying about your reputation, fair maiden, for I will make an honest woman of you."

"Give it a rest, Ray." She put her head in her hands "I'm not a slag or a groupie."

"No, you're not, you're the future Mrs Warbler. I've been waiting for you all my life," he said holding her hands in his. She looked into his eyes and saw what she was looking for.

chapter twenty-four

Ned glanced up and down the corridor and crept out of his room, slinking along to Cassy's room. Stiffening he heard Eric's voice coming toward him. He turned and rushed back into his room, breathing heavily standing against the closed door.

Form, Kate, Chardonnay and Eric strode purposefully down the corridor, Eric enthusiastically discussing the engagement party that evening. It really was the last thing on Kate and Form's minds at the moment. Chardonnay reassuringly hugged Kate. "Don't you worry about the party, leave it to us."

"Yes, leave the show to me darling, safe hands, safe hands." Eric waggled his hands in Kate's face.

"I think you two need to visit the sphere," said Chardonnay.

"Yes, yes, we do." Form and Kate nodded enthusiastically. As they turned the corner, Ray and Keily exited the stairwell to the conservatory affectionately tussling together and almost knocking Eric flying.

Maybelline and Greg standing at the top of the stairwell listened to the muffled conversation below and grimaced. "What we gonna do, shall we just balls it out?" asked Maybelline.

"We can't for f**ks sake, May! We've just watched them shagging. Shhh, we'll sneak down in a minute once they're gone." May gasped and pointed to the candy floss wisps of air curling down the stairwell from the open door. They both crouched lower and Greg slid the door almost closed. They pressed their ears to the gap.

"My future wife, my future wife!" Ray announced. Keily giggled. "I think he might even be serious you know," she stammered.

Eric's voice rang loudly. "Darlings," he crooned, "this is amazing news. I'm counting the Hello exclusive deals as we speak! Come tell us, Form and Kate have something to attend to in the conservatory, they'll follow us later, now I want to hear the gossip, the unprintable stuff!" He shooed Form and Kate into the stairwell.

May and Greg frantically turned around and then floated back to the sofa to hide behind it. Half annoyed, yet still finding the situation funny they made themselves comfy.

Form and Kate made their way straight to the sphere, holding hands tightly, excited anticipation on their faces. The ripple of shudders that followed their contact with the sphere brought a knowing smile to those that felt it.

Form and Kate held hands and smiled. Settled and seated in the sphere, Form pressed the button.

All the other hosts froze and fell silent, on pause; thirty seconds passed. As the sphere returned gently to the ground they stirred, nodding to each other as if giving approval to something.

As the sphere halted, Kate and Form fell into each other's arms, smothering kisses, groping hands, sexual tension on overdrive. Kate climbed on top of Form removing her top as she went. Rubbing her breasts across his face, taking his face in her hand she held her face close to his. "You have to fill me, I need it," she said breathily. Form had no intention of arguing with her.

Maybelline and Greg crept out from behind the sofa, silently floating to the doorway. Greg nodded over to the sphere. "If the space ship's a rockin', don't come a knocking."

Maybelline laughed loudly and then smothered her mouth, tittering.

211

Ned and Cindy stirred as Form and Kate were launched. Curled up cosily together they grinned and snuggled further. Ned yawned and stretched widely. "I feel great"

"Me too," said Cindy mirroring his moves.

"You're a wonderful, woman Cindy," Ned said casting an appreciative glance over Cindy's body stretched cat like on the bed.

"You better believe it," Cindy retorted with a flirtatious glance.

"Come with me, I've got something to show you," Ned said getting up.

"You can show it to me here if you like!"

Ned chuckled. "Oh lady, I am so going to show you that, but I want to take you to heaven, come with me." He kissed her tenderly on the lips, and they exchanged a deep look.

"I love my husband," she said.

He put his fingers to her lips. "Shh, I know you do, this is special, we both know it, don't get guilty, honey, let's just enjoy it and have a fantastic memory to share."

Cindy nodded. Ned took her gently by the hand and led her out of the room.

Kate's ruffled head emerged from the sphere. She stood naked on the edge of the sphere and luxuriated in the air. Form sat back and watched her, grinning from ear to ear. Suddenly Kate threw herself back in the sphere. "Ned and Cindy have just walked in, I heard them. They didn't see me," she quickly informed Form in a rushed whisper. Form laughed.

"What should we do?"

"Put some clothes on for a start and close the door. He's probably just giving her a quick tour. We'll hide, shh."

Cassy watched Ned and Cindy creep along the corridor together. As they turned into the stairwell she scurried over to

Leo's room, tapped and let herself in. Leo greeted her enthusiastically. "I've been waiting for you, you little minx!" Cassy giggled and joined Leo on the bed.

Cindy was as stunned as anyone when she entered the conservatory. Wrapped in the pink, fluffy electric air, she twirled around. She lay back and wallowed in the experience of floating. "This is so unreal, surreal, wotever real, really real," she laughed.

"Does it make you horny, baby?" Ned inquired with a sly grin and a wink.

Cindy ran her hands down her body. "Yes it does… Baby."

Ned made a grab for Cindy. "Come here, you sexy momma."

"Be gentle with me," she said dramatically.

Form and Kate listened to the conversation wide-eyed. "Isn't she married?" asked Form in a hushed whisper. "Yes, yes, she is, but it's all show biz I imagine," replied Kate. "Let's just close the door and keep our noses out of it," suggested Kate, Form nodded. "Yes, sounds good," as he closed the sphere.

As Eric entered the lab his gaze went straight to the table which Alison and Tinny were laying food on. "I AM STARVING!" he announced.

"Just a spot of lunch to keep your strength up," said Tinny.

"What an angel you are, Tinny," said Ray giving her a hug. "Long time no see, still as gorgeous as ever. May I introduce you to my future wife, Keily."

"Ray! Will you stop saying that!" Keily butted in sharply.

"It's true, gonna happen, you can fight it, but it's a waste of time, Keily, you are mine, all mine"

"Keily, surrender to the force!" Eric quipped

They all felt the sudden rush of energy and simultaneously shuddered. This seemed to bring Eric around. He adopted a serious posture. "All round the table, all round the table please," he called out. "Let me and Chardonnay put you in the picture while we eat."

May and Greg randomly chose a dorm room, for a bit of a clean and tidy up as May put it.

Leo and Cassy jumped with a start as they heard the door slam in the next room. "Who do you think that was?" asked Cassy.

Leo shrugged. "Dunno"

They listened to the sounds from next door. "It's May and Greg I think," Cassy said

"Let's get out of here, let me show you the space ship. It's really kooky up there, floating on music."

"Like what?"

Leo grabbed her hand. "Listen, Cassy, I am hornier than the horniest horny thing ever, and that conservatory has gotta be the place to have the ultimate sexual experience. You game?"

Cassy took a step back, and turned from him. "Not the most romantic proposal ever."

"I ain't asking you to marry me, just shag me," replied Leo.

"Oh, thanks a lot, nice one, what a charmer you are."

"Come off it, Cassy, you're just as horny, you know you are. Don't play the sanctimonious virgin."

"I'm not!"

"You're not horny or you're not sanctimonious?"

"Both."

"Liar." Leo put his arms around Cassy's waist. "Come on," he drawled. "You know you wanna.

Ned and Cindy stood at the fireplace. Cindy spent some time gazing at the sphere and soaking up the atmosphere. Ned stroked her hair and neck from behind. "Amazing isn't it, pulses through your veins." He leant forward and kissed her neck. "My veins are pulsing, wanna feel?" he whispered into her ear.

Cindy turned round to face him. He gently pushed her against the fireplace and they kissed softly groaning with pleasure. Ned slowly kissed down Cindy's neck, cleavage, opened her blouse and released one of her breasts and hungrily sucked on it. Cindy arched her back and leant into him. Her hands grasping for his belt, she undid it and let his trousers drop. His manhood standing proud, she took it in her hand and groaned loudly. Ned moaned into her breast as she held him. Ned tenderly undid Cindy's trousers too and slid them down her legs. Taking her flimsy thong with them, he cheekily kissed her groin as he knelt before her, giving her a wary glance. She smiled, he kissed it again. She took his face in her hand and guided him back to standing. "That's only for Olly to do, OK?" Ned nodded and they kissed again. Ned took Cindy's buttocks in his cupped hands and lifted her onto his manhood. She wrapped her legs around his waist and they slowly and softly pleasured each other pressed against the stone wall of the fireplace. Hands stroking, groping, pulling. Groins thrusting, grinding, moist and slippery.

Form and Kate were curled up together and dozing in the warm fuzzy serenity inside the sphere. Kate stirred. We'd better not fall asleep, they'll be looking for us, we've got things to do."

Form lazily hushed her. "Yes, yes, don't worry, I'll check and see if Ned and Cindy have gone yet."

He opened the sphere and a vibration wafted through the fireplace.

"Whoa! What was that?" cried Ned suddenly wrenched from the tender post-coital embrace he was enjoying.

Form grimaced to Kate and swiftly closed the sphere again.

Cindy scrambled her clothes together as much as she could. It is very difficult to scramble when the atmosphere makes you move as if in slow motion. "Let's get out of here!"

May and Greg were making their way back to the lab as Cindy and Ned exited the stairwell.

"Oh, hi," May greeted them "Was it your first time?" she asked Cindy.

"Pardon?" Cindy queried, unsure what Maybelline was referring to.

Ned coughed loudly.

Greg motioned his head to Ned inquisitively. Ned smiled and nodded. Greg gave him the thumbs up!

"The conservatory, amazing isn't it, this whole thing is like a dream," May replied.

"Oh yes, the conservatory, the ship, the floating, I'm not sure if I'm not on some wild drug trip," said Cindy.

"Yea, I know what you mean, we're all mad, this is all madness," said Greg

"Nothing wrong with madness, I've always liked it," said Ned.

Cautiously Form and Kate emerged from the sphere. "Coast's clear," Form said.

"Thank God for that. How embarrassing."

"I know, it's going to be difficult to look Cindy in the eye after that," said Form.

"Why Cindy, why not Ned?" asked Kate.

"Oh, don't start the battle of the sexes now, Kate. Coz she's married, that's why."

"Oh right, yes, well, her and Olly have always been very rock 'n' roll," offered Kate.

"Yes, well, maybe so, but, oh, it's not my business, is it?" said Form flatly.

Cassy and Leo watched Form and Kate make their way to the lab from a crouched position leaning round the corner. Once Form and Kate were out of sight they quickly made a dash to the stairwell, Leo removing his clothes as he climbed the stairs, Cassy giggling and picking up his cast offs as she followed behind.

"Come with me to Orgasmertron City, Cassy, let's fly on the wings of bliss," Leo grandly announced as he lunged into the pink mist already naked apart from his scarf and socks.

Cassy adopted the compulsory stunned pose when she entered the room. "Oh my God, Lordy, lordy look at this, Leo!"

Leo spun around in reckless abandon. "Soak it up, Baby, this is the trip of a lifetime, feel the air, feel the love, feel the music."

"I'm feeling," said Cassy coating and stroking herself in the air.

The lab was alive with conversation as Form and Kate entered. Everyone was crowded at the table enthusiastically tucking into Tinny's luscious spread. Eric was waving a bread stick in the air and adopting a pose.

"Oh, Form, Form, Ally told me about your entrance to the party. It's brilliant, but we, I, can make it *so* much better. I'm working on it now, don't worry, darlings, you won't have to do a thing. Leave it all to Uncle Eric!"

"Have you met the future Mrs Warbler?" Ray asked Kate.

Kate turned to Keily with eyebrows almost in her hairline.

Keily smiled and shrugged. "What can I say? He's smitten with me."

"Oh, how lovely," said Kate picking at the food on the table, trying to stop her stomach from growling and not wanting to appear rude, but she was starving!

"I thought we could make it a double engagement party," Ray offered.

Kate turned to him. "Think again, buster, this is my party!" she blurted, with a mouthful of pork pie.

"Ooer, fair enough, just an idea," he said backing away in mock terror.

"Are you being a cheapskate and trying to get out of paying for a party for me, Ray?" said Keily in an accusing tone.

"Oh, shit, I walked right into that one, didn't I, and here's me thinking I was being all romantic!"

Leo and Cassy floated in the air, rubbing their naked bodies against one another groaning and moaning deeply, enjoying every static electrically charged contact. Totally immersed in a frenzy of tactile pleasure, their bodies and faces flushed, they washed themselves in heaven. Gentle kisses all over, greeted with sighs until a kiss on the lips turned the sensual into the lustful.

Cassy roughly pushed Leo into a prone position and mounted him. Leo grinned widely. "Love it!"

Cassy leant towards Leo's face. He moved forward to kiss her. She stretched back, arms held high and ground her hips down hard on him. "Oh yes, oh yes" he drooled. Sliding forward on him again, brushing his chest with her breasts, she held her face close to his and smiled seductively, arching away from him again. He grasped her buttocks firmly and pulled her into him. They fell easily into a rhythm, thrusting, grinding, muscles taut with desire, breaths hot and fast, deep guttural moans.

Kate looked around her. This had to be the most bizarre situation possible. Here she was, being taught the dance routine for 'Prince Charming' by Maybelline, while upstairs a space ship hummed, a 'being' was in her belly (Oh now hold on, where was the 'being'? Belly? Head? Spine! Head, I think head, she

218

decided). She was having an engagement party for all the toffs in the world here tonight. Ray Warbler was dressing up as a pirate and the Prime Minister's wife was trying on a 'wench' dress assisted by Eric Ipod wearing a corset and bloomers!

Form came up behind her and put his arms around her waist, "You OK honey?"

"We're going to have to tear up any rule books we had after this, Form. How do you feel about that?" she asked.

"Can't say," he shrugged. "Everything's so bizarre, I think there'll be a few songs written about it and maybe a film perhaps. They will make things clearer for us," Form said lightly.

Spent Leo and Cassy lay draped on the sofa.

"That was amazing," said Cassy.

"I told you it would be, you were amazing, God, you are hot."

"Yea, I know." Cassy gave a big sigh and laughed.

"I want more," stated Leo.

Cassy stroked his lip with her finger. "Another time!" and she gathered her clothes together dressing as she made her way to the door. Leo whined, "Aww, no fair!"

As the door closed behind Leo, the cherry picker engine hummed into action and it was lowered to the floor. Before it came to a halt the door opened and James stepped out, carrying Amy in his arms, and floated easily down.

Amy affectionately stroked James's hair. "Well, that was an experience!"

James chuckled. "Quite a show!"

chapter twenty-five

James entered the lab quietly. He and Amy stood just inside the door and watched the hustle and bustle of the room.

Colin and Alison were showing Eric a selection of large wicker trunks full of costumes they had brought down from the recording studio stores. Alison was parading some of them proudly as she had made them for a video The Rolling Stones had shot here ten years earlier.

James shook his head. Was there no end to the talents of that woman, he thought fondly.

Even Samuel, Roger, Tom and Romme were engrossed in the preparations for the grand entrance 'show' Eric had decided to create.

Ray, Ned and Leo were all holding guitars and practising strumming and strutting in time to the tune like old friends.

Form turned round and saw James and Amy.

"James! Hi!" he stammered.

A hush ensued and everyone stared at James and Amy.

James raised his hands. "Fear not, fellow friends of the cosmic, I am one of your own," he said dramatically.

"And me!" piped up Amy.

"Yes, my dear, and you."

James scanned the room. "Time for an explanation, I think!"

"Well, if it's not too much bother," said Colin sarcastically.

"Colin!" Alison chastised him.

"Colin, you have done an excellent job. It's not a bad reflection on you that you didn't know. It's been my job to check security remained tight and you definitely did a great job. Best undercover for a spy is to appear a risk, don't you think?"

"Ahhh," echoed throughout the lab as everyone twigged James's role in things.

Tea and coffee were made and they all huddled round the table. They came to the conclusion that keeping everyone's presence secret, while still holding the engagement party which it was far too late to cancel, would seem suspicious if they did it and anyway was unrealistic. Announcing everyone in this dramatic entrance seemed an excellent way of diverting attention away from what was happening in the conservatory. As long as they kept people away from the south wing all should be fine.

They were all aware that they were waiting for something. Samuel confirmed that the sphere was sending out massive signals, but as yet they had not had any readings indicating a reply or that the messages had even reached their source.

"How long do you think we are going to have to wait?" asked Greg.

"Your guess is as good as mine. Could be days, could be months," Samuel replied.

"No way!" groaned Leo.

"We can't be here for months, James!" May turned to him slightly panicked.

He smiled. "It won't be long, don't worry."

May calmed.

Alison, forever practical, said, "It's four o'clock, time for everyone to get their costumes and go and get ready nice and leisurely."

This suggestion was met with approval.

"All meet up at Form's suite seven o'clock?" James suggested.

"Where?" asked Cassy.

"Don't worry, sweetie, we'll collect you," Tinny reassured her.

"Sounds good," said Eric. "Now, do you all know your moves?"

Stretching out from opposite ends of the bubble-filled bath, eyes closed, Form and Kate held a lazy conversation about the goings on so far today.

"How do you feel with the alien possession situation?" Kate asked.

"Blimey, hadn't really thought of it as being possessed," he replied. "I'm OK with it, I don't feel much different, just confident, well, I suppose that's quite a major change really!"

"I feel bad lying in this bath knowing Maybelline's making do with the dorm rooms."

"Oh don't, she's stayed in much worse. Alison's sorting them out rooms in the main house for tonight so she'll be fine."

Kate was reassured by this and they returned to silent slumber.

Kate need not have worried. Maybelline, Cassy, Cindy and Keily were enjoying a girly pampering session, going through the dance moves and doing each other's make-up, like the consummate professionals they were.

Eric was taking a luxurious bath as Ned, Ray, Leo and Greg huddled together on a dorm bed and shared in intimate detail the sexual antics that had taken place in the conservatory. Greg informed Ray that he and May had been behind the sofa, to guffaws of laughter from Ned and Leo. Ned received much ribbing about Cindy, but brushed it aside.

"She's amazing, don't make judgments, it's all cool," was all he would say.

"I'm gonna marry Keily," announced Ray.

"Yea, good idea," said Leo. "She'll be good for you"

"Yea, I know."

"Cassy's cool," mumbled Leo.

"Cassy's hot!" said Greg.

Leo grinned. "Yea, Cassy's hot!"

Form stirred from a deep slumber, hearing a phone ringing. It seemed far off in the distance, getting louder and louder as he woke. He suddenly jerked, splashing water everywhere and startling Kate awake.

Form clambered out of the bath and stumbled to the phone.

"Hello."

"Mr Form, sir," said Colin.

"Yes, Colin, what is it?" Form asked.

"Mr David is here. I thought I ought to inform you."

Form looked out of the window and noted the hustle and bustle below as the staff were making preparations for the arrival of hundreds of guests in only an hour or so. The driveway adorned with flowers and lights, swept out of eyesight. A glorious white silk awning extended from the main entrance all the way down the wide steps to the drive; it shimmered in the light breeze.

"Thank you, Colin, send him on up. How are things going your end? It must be mayhem."

"Not at all, Mr Form, sir, everything under control. We've had plenty of practice. We go onto automatic pilot."

"It all looks lovely from here, Colin, well done."

Form hung up the phone and called to Kate, "David's on his way up, better get some clothes on, you floozy!"

David knocked and sauntered in, swaggering in his tuxedo and doing a twirl as he walked toward Form in his dressing gown. Form mirrored the twirl with a laugh.

"Are we ready to *PARTEE?*" David yelled.

Form laughed. Kate called from the bathroom, "We are ready to *PARTEE,*" as she wriggled into a lacy basque.

David was bouncing, pacing up and down. "God, I'm like a kid going to his first tea party, dunno why!"

"David, have we got some surprises for you, my boy!" said Form "You are totally gonna flip out."

"What?" cried David. "I knew something was up. I'm sensitive to vibes. What's going on?"

Form grinned wryly. 'Sensitive to vibes' ha!

"You better sit your botty down, David, have I got a superscoop for you!"

Kate called from the dressing room. "Wait, I want to see his face, I'll just be a minute."

David grimaced at Form. Form shrugged and grinned.

Kate dramatically swung the door open and draped herself on the frame. She was dressed in a rather gaudy 'pirate' tart outfit, a striped bodice, petticoats and feathers in her hair.

David gave a shrill wolf whistle. Kate bowed. "Thank you, kind sir." Form wandered over to Kate and slid his arm around her waist. "Nice, very nice indeed!"

David could not contain his excitement. "Ray Warbler and the Granger brothers and Maybelline! Man, Form, this is way off the scale of unreal." He clapped his hands together as he paced up and down.

"David, this needs to go on film," said Form.

"Too bloody right it does," said David.

"I know it's a bit last minute, but can you be our camera man? We need someone to get the crowd in the right place and we need a camera man, someone we can trust, paparazzi all over the place already."

David nodded. "Yea, man, no problem, 'nuff said." He looked around him. "Do you have a camera?"

Kate laughed. "Not right here at this moment. I'll call Colin and get him to bring one up."

"I better get changed too," said Form going into the dressing room. "I'm Prince Charming after all."

"I don't get how the pirate outfits fit in with Prince Charming," mused David.

"Wrong video for the song but only a music dweeb like you would notice," laughed Kate. "Nearest we could manage with such short notice. Alison made a whole ton of pirate outfits for the Rolling Stones once, I bet this bodice is famous!"

A knock on the door. Ned popped his head round. "Are we in the right place?"

"Oh my God, Ned Granger!" blurted David.

"Yes, come on in. Form's just getting dressed. You look great," Kate said as she ushered Ned in followed by Cindy, Cassy, Maybelline, Leo and Greg.

"Ray's on his way. He's coming in the lift with Samuel."

David introduced himself to everyone as David, lifelong friend of the lord and master, which raised a few polite smiles.

"I will be your cameraman for this evening," he announced.

Greg pulled him to one side and began quizzing him on film types and lighting. David attempted to bluff for a bit and then admitted he had no clue about filming, but would do his best. Greg was not impressed.

Eric, Chardonnay and Keily entered the room, Chardonnay and Keily striding in ruffling their skirts and pointing at the other girls. They went into a huddle comparing outfits. Ray followed Samuel's chair into the room waving a 'hooked' hand in the air, making 'pirate' oo's and arrragh's .

Colin entered the busy room with three camera cases flung over his shoulder and searched David out. Greg followed Colin and began checking out the cameras. He chose one for David, the one least likely to get messed up, he announced, filling David with dread. David got behind the camera and immediately felt more comfortable. This was a 'happening' and he was going to film it; this was history in the making.

The phone rang, and Form absently picked it up. "Samuel, it's Roger," he called across the room.

"Samuel, the monitors have gone wild," Roger said excitedly into the phone.

Colin suddenly began to usher David out of the room. "You need to check out the lighting in the hall," he said as they exited the room.

Samuel turned from the phone to relay the information to the others only to be confronted with them all standing frozen, in a daze.

"They're here," said Form quietly.

"We better all get back to the conservatory, PDQ," said Greg.

The first few guests began arriving as David made his way down the main stairway into the entrance hall, camera in hand, turning around, checking lights as he walked.

He waved a greeting to the guests. "This is going to be a night you will never forget!" he assured them. They laughed politely and moved off into the inner lounge.

"Just you wait and see, you stuck up morons," he muttered to himself.

chapter twenty-six

They all dashed as fast as they could to the conservatory. As they climbed the stairwell they could see the wisps of air emerging from under the door, only now it was blue. Leo, who was leading the group, halted. Maybelline behind him peered over his shoulder at the mist. She tutted and gave him a shove in the back and they all carried on eagerly.

Leo didn't launch himself into the air this time. He entered the conservatory very cautiously; the air felt lighter than before, but still highly charged. Tiny little sparks flew off them as they congregated around the fireplace. A motley crew of pirates and their wenches, feathers and eye patches, accompanied by one Prince Charming in a silver silk suit, ruffles and sequins galore. They stood silently looking at the sphere which had also taken on a blue hue and was humming loudly.

"Any volunteers?" asked Samuel as he emerged from the lift, Roger and Tom walking behind him.

"Any suggestions?" Maybelline and Cindy retorted together, and then giggled.

"Draw straws?" suggested Keily.

"You got any straws?" asked Leo.

"You spotted the fatal flaw in my plan," she countered.

Ned stepped forward. "How about me an' Leo?"

"We're not paired off together, you twonk," said Leo.

"I believe Form and Kate need to go first," Chardonnay announced.

"Only fair for Prince Charming to lead the way," agreed May.

"Thanks," Form responded.

Form took Kate by the hand. As they climbed into the sphere a huge hum erupted, the sound wave pushing the others standing around the fireplace backwards slightly. Cindy, losing her footing, tumbled into Cassy, who in turn tumbled into Leo, who caught her and assisted her to regain her balance, leaving Cindy to fall to the floor.

Ned was by her side in a second. Cindy sat on the floor, holding her hand up to Ned "Real gentleman your brother is!" she said sarcastically to Ned.

"Two hands, lady, only two hands!" Leo returned.

They hushed their banter as the sphere closed, eyes fixed on the sphere, breath suitably bated.

The sphere took a second or two powering up, the humming increasing and then shot at speed right up the chimney, sending a further blast which knocked everyone onto their bottoms this time into the room. They peered into the fireplace, which seemed suddenly like a black hole.

The sphere had shot right up to the top of the chimney, blocking any light, sitting like a plug in the hole. A stream of blue/white pulses shot skyward.

People arriving noticed the sky suddenly pulsing with light and looked around to see where it came from.

"What was that?" asked a rather regal lady.

"Probably one of their wacky inventions," her partner responded, a touch of distaste in his voice.

She rolled her eyes and nodded.

Another rush of air swept from the fireplace, it became light again and the sphere bobbed close to the ground again.

The sphere had barely halted when Form and Kate emerged with purpose.

Twitchy with energy Kate told the others, "Right, action stations, in your pairs, as fast as possible, not much time." She put her arm around Cindy's shoulder and guided her to the sphere.

Cindy was clearly nervous, Kate patted her reassuringly "Don't worry, it's nice!"

"Really?"

"Really," Kate replied.

Ned and Cindy climbed into the sphere. This time everyone braced themselves for the blast as the sphere shot up the chimney.

As the sphere landed again they drew around it as it powered down. Cindy was in tears as she got out. Cassy and May ran to her side.

"What's up?" Cassy enquired.

"You OK?" May asked putting her arm around Cindy's shoulder.

"It's lovely," sobbed Cindy. "Don't mind me, I'm just being daft."

The men crowded round Ned asking questions. Form was slightly nonplussed that they hadn't asked him anything!

Romme bowled into the conservatory, puffing and panting, waving his hand in the air to get their attention.

"Outside," he puffed pointing toward the windows. "Everyone can see it, it's lighting up the sky!"

"Shit!" exclaimed Ned. "Right, hurry it up here, no time to waste, one pair in, one pair out, let's get this done." He took control and pushed Ray toward the sphere. "Time for talk later."

"No need to panic," interjected Greg. "Just tell them you're testing a light show for later. People expect the unexpected here, they won't bat an eyelid."

Samuel and Roger nodded. "Good point!" Roger said

Ray and Keily inside it, the sphere shot up the chimney again, again catching them unawares and everyone staggered to remain upright against the blast of air.

James decided to take things in hand. "If we distract everyone as soon as possible, no one will ask questions." He took Cindy's hand. "If everyone makes their way to Form's suite as soon as they've done here, we can go straight into the 'grand entrance' and this will be forgotten."

Given instruction, Ned, Cindy, Form, Kate, Ray and Keily made swiftly off, flushed faces and slightly breathless, patting each other on the back and exchanging 'knowing' glances but not saying much.

As they strode along the corridor at a hefty pace, suddenly they all froze, paused motionless for thirty seconds.

"Lovely, just lovely," murmured Cindy. May and Kate either side of her hugged her tightly.

David mooched among the growing crowd of visitors, waving his camera, taking the occasional bit of film of any particularly pretty ladies and instructing them to 'hold onto their hats' later. Floor show of all floor shows going on, here, tonight, making history, he commented time and time again. The news that there was going to be some sort of spectacular 'happening' spread through the crowd and as people entered commenting on the lights in the sky outside, the atmosphere grew and grew with excitement. The 'beautiful' people swanned around sipping on the champagne being offered, discussing the different possibilities for this anticipated event.

David looked up at the landing and saw Roger, Samuel and Tom positioning themselves with a view of the stairs. David waved to them. Tom made his way down the stairs toward him. "Get ready, two minutes!" David gave him the thumbs up and Tom turned around and returned to Samuel's side.

The lights went out, deep bass music boomed, a light came on at the top of the stairs. Form stood upright and proud, head high, chest out, looking every bit the Prince Charming. He strode forward, one arm raised and behind him Kate, Cassy and Maybelline came into the spotlight.

The crowd gasped as they immediately recognised Maybelline and Cassy.

Mimicking Form's moves, the girls stepped down onto the next stair, Chardonnay, Keily, (a very smiley) Amy and Cindy came into the light, strutting proudly in their pirate wench outfits.

The crowd below began to applaud. David was beaming, down on one knee at the bottom of the stairs with the camera. "Awesome, this is awesome!"

The loud deep bell tolls of the introduction was joined by the strum of guitars and Ned, Ray and Leo strode into view.

The room erupted. Women screamed, gasps swept the hall, jaws dropped. David involuntarily jumped up, quickly returning to his kneeling pose at the bottom of stairs, highly embarrassed to find that he was so excited and had a huge erection, making it difficult to manoeuvre. No one noticed.

Behind Ned, Ray and Leo, strode Greg, Eric and James brandishing pirate cutlasses over their heads with panache.

The crowd cheered, many joining in the well known moves and singing along.

Form led them strutting down the stairs. Behind him the girls broke into the practised dance routine, twisting, turning changing places, smooth moves as if they had been doing it for years.

chapter twenty-seven

(The Mothership)

Inside the huge cavernous pearlescent chamber, light tinkling bells could be heard.

With each tinkle a form appeared at the smooth shiny white desk at the head of the room, slightly raised or perhaps floating. Although the chamber was almost blindingly white, the atmosphere felt dark.

The head of the Council rose, eight feet in height, not including the mass of white wispy tendrils that curled from his head. He picked up an ornate stick in his long white claw like hand and pointed it toward the forlorn group standing before him.

The ghostly figures shuffled forward, crouching subserviently.

"FAIL," boomed the Councillor.

The figures crouched further.

A slightly smaller member of the Council rose. "Explain."

One of the group moved forward.

"We apologise for our failure, Councillor, if we had more time!"

"Two hundred years is quite long enough for any school project, Maraliss, as you well know," replied the smaller Councillor.

"We got here very late in their development, in our defence. Much damage had already been done. They had gone down the primitive route right from the start!"

The Councillors exchanged glances and nodded. "So you had some repair work to do," said the head Councillor.

"They had learnt to talk before they learnt to listen. They are obsessed with something they call money. They speak a multitude of different languages. No one trusts anyone else. These were major hurdles, Councillor! We worked really hard!"

"Stay there, we will give this some consideration," the head Councillor announced.

With elegant little tinkling noises they evaporated and the group were left alone.

They turned to each other and hugged, stroking each other's tendrils.

"Nice to be back to normal again," said Maraliss.

"What a pig of a project," remarked Glavil.

"No way we're going to pass, so that means a quick trip home and another project," Pertenli moaned.

"We'll be able to wrap the next one up in fifty years, no problem," declared Maraliss. "After this lot, we should be able to awaken any species. Once the keys come into play this lot will find the answers. It's just taking them forever to do it!"

"I thought we had it with that Lennon bloke," said Glavil.

"Yes, me too," said Maraliss.

"They just weren't listening." Darlity shook his head disappointedly.

"Lovely to be back in my own body at last," said Glavil. Stroking her long white claws down her wispy body, running them through her tendrils, she stretched and launched herself into flight.

"Oh, it's been so long..." she gently swooped around the chamber.

This appeared to be a good idea as the others all joined her, sighing with pleasure.

"I can't believe we are going home at last," said Pertenli

Livintol began to sing as she swooped high to the ceiling, a haunting lilting musical sigh. The others all joined in, obviously singing a favourite or at least well known tune.

At the first indication of a 'tinkle', the group reformed in front of the desk. The Councillors reappeared; the head was holding a large heavy bound book.

"We have given your case some consideration and some information has come to my attention," he announced tapping the book.

Curiously the group edged closer.

"We may have marked you harshly," he continued.

The group cheered up slightly, hopeful.

"Apparently there was an abandoned project here before. They were recalled due to the Quado Incident."

The group nodded their understanding. The Quado Incident had put a halt to many of their projects for hundreds of years.

"The previous students only stayed for about forty years, just over 2,000 years ago. They made a good start but weren't able to leave any keys behind to carry it on for them."

"That explains a lot," Maraliss piped in quite abruptly.

"Yes, yes indeed," said the head, slightly embarrassed.

Pertenli pondered for a moment.

"There is a possibility that the host of the team leader from the previous expedition might have been killed!"

"What makes you think that?" asked the Council head.

"There was a religion they used on Earth, a belief system, very primitive, but it was based around a so-called prophet 2000 or so years ago. They publicly executed him."

"Yes!" interrupted Maraliss "It caused massive divides, believers, non-believers, wars were fought over it! They are so primitive, they killed their own kind for not sharing the same belief!"

Glavil raised an arm to gain the Councillor's attention. The Councillors acknowledged Glavil and she moved forward.

"This species didn't have only one religion based on the prophet. There were many, all differing in their interpretation of the information left behind. They have a variety of books which they refer to. These beings only live for an average of seventy years so the books have been written by a variety of different people, none of whom were even hosts!"

The Councillors gave this some consideration.

The group exchanged hopeful glances.

"The previous expedition's report was minimal and we believed had caused little or no impact. Apparently we were mistaken."

"I can recall parts of one of the books makes references to wondrous miracles, walking on water being one of them, Council!" Livintol added.

"Yes, we can see now how that might have made your task immensely difficult, pity, such a pity. The report claimed that they had made little or no impact and that they had not drawn attention to themselves. Levitation prior to even basic understanding of energy waves is such a foolish thing to do!" said the head Councillor.

"We will have to have words with Jesuneme; he was in charge of that expedition. If we had known about the levitation he would never have got the Tyletic project!" he continued.

"We've left six keys," said Livintol lightly.

"Good job," the smaller Councillor said.

The Councillors huddled together again, and an agreement was met. The Councillors rose lightly in unison, tendrils erect, an aura of light emanating from them.

The group solemnly awaited the Council's conclusion.

"We believe that, under the circumstances, considering the report of the previous students, and bearing in mind you managed to leave so many keys, we will give you a passing grade."

The group let out an excited shrill whine, which made their tendrils wave wildly.

"Bottom grade pass!" the Councillor emphasised. "It'll take them another hundred years with only six keys to guide them, but this planet will get there, so, well done, you did your best."

chapter twenty-eight

The party was going with a swing; the grand entrance had blown the crowd away. To some people it had seemed like their idols had almost floated down the stairs.

David excitedly tapped the video camera. "Scoop of the year here, scoop of the year, Pondlife and Warbler united, who would have believed it?" he said again and again to anyone who would listen. People nodded in agreement, his excitement being mirrored by all. He searched Form out in the crowd. "Who would have believed you would be on MTV?" he announced to Form.

Form gave him a puzzled look. "What?"

"This video is going to be all over the world by the end of next week. You'll be a star of MTV," David laughed.

Form smiled. "Nothing surprises me nowadays."

Music played in the big hall, the hum of conversation was lively. The pirates and their wenches mingled with the crowd, signing the occasional napkin, shirt or arm. They glided through the crowd laughing, and enthusing with people as they went.

After an hour or so Form and Kate found themselves watching the party from the landing.

James tapped Form on the shoulder making him jump slightly.

"Sorry to startle you," James apologised.

"Oh, it's you, James!" Form smiled at Amy standing behind James.

James put his arms around Amy and leant over the banister slightly to watch the crowd. "Great party," he said.

"Most amazing day of my life," said Form in a slightly dazed tone.

James placed his hand on Amy's stomach and patted it. He nodded to Form's hand also resting on Kate's stomach. "We have the keys to our future in our hands."

Form and Kate turned to look at him, a questioning look on their faces.

James leant forward and made a sweeping gesture over the crowd.

"Here in this house, we have all the brains and power needed to rewrite the whole of the rule book and Form, that is what we are going to do. Don't think this is the end, this is only the beginning."

"Of what? Beginning of what?"

"The next chapter, Form," said Kate, looking at her stomach and stroking it.

"You think you're pregnant?" he asked her.

She nodded.

"Since when?"

"Since this afternoon," she said with a coy grin.

Form picked her up and spun her round. "A baby, a Daddy, blimey, definitely a new chapter."

Amy snuggled up to James. "We're going to be a Mummy and a Daddy too!"

"I believe the 'beings' left us some gifts!" said James.

"You think so?" asked Form.

"More a sense of knowing," replied James.

"What else do you know?" Kate asked.

"I know that we have in our possession the answer to the world's energy problems. We can get rid of oil, coal, gas!" He snapped his fingers. "Just like that, but we are going to have a struggle. Not everyone's going to like this."

"Oh my God, do you mean the sphere works without the aliens?" gasped Form.

James nodded enthusiastically.

"Show me," said Form.

The conservatory was dark and cold, a drastic change from only a couple of hours ago. The sphere sat in the fireplace, dull and lifeless.

"This doesn't look too hopeful," said Kate.

"Oh ye of little faith," said James.

He walked over to the table and pressed a key on the organ. A long low tone emitted, the sphere hummed into life immediately and the door opened. Slight wisps of white mist had replaced the thick pink candy floss from before and the sphere bobbed lightly.

They circled the sphere. "Can we make more of these?" Form asked.

"Easier than making a car, now we have it worked out," James confirmed proudly. "No more pollution, no more road accidents, no more roads!" he said.

"Form, you are going to have so much fun, honey," said Kate. "So many rule books to rewrite." Form smiled. "An interesting project indeed!"

"You want to take it for its maiden voyage?" James asked.

"Now?" Kate was surprised at the offer.

"Yes, now, no time like the present. World's press at your door, all the power people and brains of Britain in attendance. Good place to launch a brave new world I think!" said James.

Kate and Form cautiously climbed into the sphere. Sliding a CD into the slot, the vibrations increased. James poked his head in. "One small step and all that," he said.

"Thanks," Kate and Form responded as the door closed. They looked at each other and grasped hands. Form pushed the button.

Slowly and steadily this time the sphere rose up the chimney. As they emerged from the top, Form and Kate could see through the shell to the starlit night sky coming toward them.

Form rolled his hand across the panel and the sphere halted. He shrugged at Kate. "Don't think for one minute that just because I'm a man, I know how to drive this."

Kate smiled. "Believe me, Form, I have faith in you."

As they glided over the iron gates of the estate the flash of paparazzi cameras shimmered like moonlight on a lake.